I0578604

AMETHYST

Mage

OTHER BOOKS BY DOROTHY DREYER

Phoenix Descending

Paragon Rising

Cauldron of Ash

Christmas in Silverwood

THE EMPIRE OF THE LOTUS SERIES

Crimson Mage

Copper Mage

Golden Mage

Emerald Mage

Sapphire Mage

Amethyst Mage

Diamond Mage

Amethyst

Mage

Empire of the Lotus

Book Six

DOROTHY DREYER

*For faith that the world will heal
and be a better place*

As the Akutake comet nears, the disruption of magic has come at the most inopportune time.

The sanctuary of the mages has been compromised. Not only is their safety at risk, but the location of the arcane daggers is a heartbeat away from being discovered by the Pishacha.

With the war's showdown on the horizon, the elite mages are grasping at straws in their attempt to stop the enemy from unleashing their evil god and his plan to end the world.

In the dreamy vale of beeches
Fair and faint is woven mist,
And the river's orient reaches
Are the palest amethyst.
– Lucy Maud Montgomery

The legend goes …

The ancient deity Kashmeru knew only one true love—the Lotus empress Lakshmi, who in his eyes possessed all beauty and grace the universe could hold. Their hearts called to one another, a hold so strong that neither one could deny the bond. But Lakshmi knew that Kashmeru's spirit was not pure, for an evil dwelled within his soul, a wickedness so corrupt that it could destroy the universe.

And when she denied him her love, destroying the universe was the very thing he vowed to do.

Throughout the centuries, their reincarnations were drawn to one another, but the outcome was always the same: Lakshmi would never give Kashmeru her heart.

To put an end to his constant chase, the Empire of the Lotus defeated Kashmeru and sealed him in a tomb using mage powers, where he would remain trapped …

… until the Council of the Seven could secure the blood of the Lotus empress to set him free.

THE SEVEN HOUSES OF MAGES

Crimson: earth, stability, survival, security.

Copper: water, ice, pleasure, guilt.

Golden: fire, willpower, shame.

Emerald: air, wind, heart, love, grief.

Sapphire: throat, sound, truth, lies.

Amethyst: vision, sight, illusions, secrets.

Diamond: spirituality, emotion, virtue, integrity.

One

The breeze that blew over the meadow was unusually warm. It made Karina think of the swamp—their home—and she knew her grandmother would have been pleased.

Karina swept her dark hair out of her face as she continued to consecrate the meadow—a piece of land on

Mr. Kitaro's property—with her mixture of sandalwood, patchouli, and jasmine oils. She repeated the blessing as she paced the ground surrounding her grandmother's grave. Once the blessing was complete, Jae and Shiro lowered the satin cocoon that was wrapped around Amalia's body, placing the deceased swamp witch in her grave.

Karina was the first to toss a handful of earth onto her grandmother's body. She did so with a tightened jaw and a heavy heart. Steadying her breaths, she forced herself not to break down. Not now. She had a ritual she needed to complete before she could allow herself to let the grief crawl in.

Darshana, the wise guru who led the mages, followed suit, gently throwing dirt upon the silk cocoon. She stood back, gazing upon the corpse of her lost friend, and closed her eyes as wind played with her long, white braid.

The others soon fell in line. Once they'd all had their turn, Jae and Shiro filled the grave. Watching her grandmother slowly disappearing beneath the soil, Karina took deep, heavy breaths and prepared herself for the incantation.

It was as if any sense of happiness or joy was being buried along with her grandmother. Her heart felt like a stone in her chest. It was a struggle just to stand. But she'd made a promise, and she intended to keep it.

Once the grave was filled, Mr. Kitaro—the Sacred Key who had accompanied the mages for much of their journey—handed each of the elite mages a candle. The mages spread out, equidistant from each other, surrounding the grave. Darshana moved away to stand beside Mr. Kitaro, and Karina, with a trembling breath, gave them a nod.

Closing her eyes, Karina recited the words of the incantation her grandmother had taught her. When she got through all the verses once, she opened her eyes and spread out her arms.

Each of the six mages held their candles secure in their left hands as they held out their right, palms facing Amalia's grave.

Karina began the incantation again. She would have to repeat it until the transfer of power was complete. Her grandmother's witch powers would first return to the earth, which was bonded with her magic. The incantation would pull those powers from the consecrated earth and guide them to Karina, who would then absorb her grandmother's magic and combine it with her own. The mages served as a power booster, the pull of their elements guiding as much magic as possible to its new home base.

Amalia had said even one mage involved in the spell would supply enough power to amplify the transfer. Penny—the elite amethyst mage—was still missing, but Karina's spell was still empowered immensely by the remaining six elites.

It was the red glow of Mayhara's power—the power of the elite crimson mage—which reached the soil of Amalia's grave first. Mayhara's long, dark waves danced around her lovely oval face, the wind causing the ends of her hair to play with her full lips.

The crimson particles were next joined by the copper glow of Shiro's power—the power of the elite copper mage. The glow mirrored the copper tips of his slightly disheveled black hair. Though Shiro stood with squared shoulders and a solid stance, there was a softness in his eyes—a sadness—that Karina couldn't miss.

The red and orange flow of magic now swirled with

the golden glow of Salina's particles. The elite golden mage had her eyes narrowed as the wind tousled her golden-highlighted curls against the dark skin of her high cheekbones.

Loni—the elite emerald mage—pushed out her powers, the glowing green particles floating in to join the red, orange, and gold. Sweat glistened at her temples, dampening the black hair framing her face. Karina wasn't sure what demons Loni was struggling with, but she suspected Loni was doing her best to conquer them.

The bright blue glow of Jae's sapphire particles swept in and spiraled around the wave of the other magical molecules, joining the surge as the massive collection of magic entered the ground. Jae was the newest elite, having inherited the station when their friend Kamal had been killed. But Jae had another connection to the prophecy that linked the two ancient deities responsible for the war that could end the world. Jae's sister, Naree, was also the reincarnation of the divine goddess Lakshmi. Of all the mages, Jae must have had the most intense personal struggle with this war.

The last mage to infuse her powers into the strain was

Yuki. She was the youngest elite mage, and as a diamond mage, also one of the rarest. Yuki looked so small, her auburn hair coming loose from her hairband, and wind made her black blouse and skirt thrash around her petite form.

Karina recited the lines of the incantation once more, raising her hands higher and opening her mind to receive the flow of magic.

It started slowly, a mild weakness in her legs. She forced herself to stand straight and hold her stance, fearing that she'd crumple to the ground if she gave in. Her body felt as if it were being hit with flashes of extreme hot and cold, and she found it difficult to breathe as lightheadedness set in.

Tunnel vision caused her to focus on the bright light surfacing from her grandmother's grave. The glittering white light hovered over the grave for a moment and then seemed to be sucked into Karina's skin. Tiny pinpricks covered her body. She heard a ringing in her ears, and the wind picked up violently, the blast of it causing her eyes to water.

And somewhere in her head, she could swear she heard

her grandmother's voice, but she couldn't make out the words.

The flames of the candles each of the mages carried went out all at once, and Karina felt every muscle in her body tense.

The wind suddenly died, and Karina could feel a warm glow in her chest—a glow that seemed to slowly grow and expand until it filled every inch of her being.

Is this it? she wondered. *Is the transfer complete?*

A gasp from Loni snapped her out of her shock. Karina turned to see Loni gaping at a figure just out of her line of vision.

"Penny?" Salina said, shaking her head, her eyes wide. Karina turned to see if it was, indeed, their long-lost amethyst mage, but the movement and the shift of balance overwhelmed her, and she felt herself falling to the ground.

Two

For a moment, Mayhara was frozen. She couldn't get her mind to wrap around the fact that Penny stood there, not fifty meters away from her. She was sure it was her. She had the same black, wavy hair, the same intense gaze, as if she could see things no one else could. She wore what Mayhara remembered her wearing when she last saw her, except a bit more disheveled. Unless Penny had a twin, it had to be her. Mayhara's eyes narrowed as doubt circled her. Could Penny really be in the meadow with them?

She flinched as Loni ran past her, shocking her out of her stupor. The second Loni pulled Penny into an embrace, Mayhara knew it couldn't be an illusion.

"Penny," Mayhara called. Her legs carried her forward before she could even catch her breath.

In her peripheral vision, she could see Shiro rushing to check on Karina, who'd crumpled to the ground after the transferal spell. If Mayhara could split herself in two, she would make her other self join Shiro to make sure Karina was all right. But her first instinct was to find out how Penny had escaped from the Pishacha's grasp.

Loni had just released Penny when Mayhara reached them. Mayhara threw her arms around Penny and squeezed her. Penny seemed stiff, not returning the embrace. Mayhara realized Penny hadn't returned Loni's embrace, either.

She's either in shock or is frozen with trauma from what happened to her, Mayhara thought.

She took a step back and looked Penny over. Aside from a bandage wrapped around one of her hands, she seemed to be okay. "It's really you."

Jae, Yuki, and Salina were soon beside her, their expressions of confusion reflecting her own.

Glancing over her shoulder, she spotted Shiro, Darshana, and Mr. Kitaro attempting to prop up the still-unconscious Karina.

"What happened?" Yuki asked Penny, placing a hand on her arm. "How did you escape?"

Penny's eyes were wide and unblinking as she glanced around at the mages surrounding her.

"You're trembling." Jae removed his jacket and wrapped it around Penny's shoulders. He nodded at the rest of the group. "Let's get her inside. Yuki, maybe you can make her a tea. I think she's in shock. We can sort everything out in the house."

Mayhara instinctively stepped to the other side of Penny so she and Yuki could lead her to the house. In a whirlwind of activity, the group made its journey. Jae helped carry Karina, seeing as she hadn't yet woken up. Penny's eyes scanned the area as they walked, obviously unfamiliar with the territory.

It seemed a grueling effort, but once they were inside, Mayhara let out a breath of relief. Jae and Shiro placed Karina on the couch in the main room, and Yuki swiftly had water boiling for tea. Loni led Penny to one of the comfortable chairs in the main room, and Salina fetched a blanket to cover her trembling legs. The rest of the mages either stood around her or sat on the carpet near her feet.

"I'm so glad you're all right," Loni said, her eyes red as tears threatened to spill.

"How did you find us?" Mayhara asked, curling her feet underneath her on the carpet.

Penny opened her mouth as if to speak but simply looked around at everyone with a confused expression.

"Give her some time." Darshana wrung her hands as she watched Penny. "She's undoubtedly suffered a lot of stress and needs a minute to breathe."

Mayhara glanced at Karina, who was still passed out on the couch. Shiro had set a wet cloth on her forehead. Mayhara wasn't sure when he'd had the time to fetch it, but in that moment, everything seemed surreal.

Yuki came into the room holding a steaming cup. She

tentatively approached Penny, her eyes searching her face. "Penny?"

Penny slowly turned her head and looked up at Yuki. At first, she only frowned. Yuki's brows were raised with anticipation. And then, Penny blinked quickly, as if waking from her trance, and reached up to take the teacup.

"Thank you," Penny said.

Mayhara felt a collective sigh of relief release from the group.

They gave Penny a moment as she sipped her tea. Mayhara felt as if goosebumps were exploding all over her body. She had so many questions but knew she'd need to wait until Penny was ready to answer them.

"Let us know if you need anything," Salina said, her voice a gentle whisper.

Penny swallowed and set the teacup on the blanket covering her legs. "To be honest, I'm not a hundred percent sure how I got here. It was like I was drawn here. Like a magnet. I reached out with my mind to Darshana, knowing she'd have the strongest connection because of meditation. And then I just followed the pull."

"I'm glad your powers didn't give you any trouble,"

Mayhara said.

Penny stopped mid-sip and lowered her cup. "What do you mean?"

"Oh." Mayhara sat up straighter. "You don't know about the comet's effect."

"Yes." Darshana ran her fingers down her long braid. "It's something that came to me as I was meditating. Trying to find you, actually. Apparently, the closer the comet gets, the more it interferes with mage powers. Shiro has experienced it. And so has Jae. Salina's had trouble getting her fire to hold as well."

"My feel of the ground doesn't seem as strong as it normally does," Mayhara added.

Penny visibly swallowed. "Oh. That's… troubling."

"To say the least." Loni clicked her tongue.

Yuki crossed her arms. "Not good news when we need all the power we can harness to keep Kashmeru at bay."

Penny dropped her gaze to her lap. She seemed to be calculating something in her head. "No. I suppose not."

"Like I said," Mayhara put in as she relaxed her shoulders, "I'm glad your powers didn't give you any trouble."

"But how did you escape?" Salina asked. "The last we saw, Naree had you captive, and you disappeared with the Pishacha."

"Leaving the chief of police dead on the floor," Loni added.

Penny nodded as she raised the teacup again. She took a long, slow sip, her gaze far away. Mayhara figured Penny was reliving the scene in her head.

"I passed out," Penny continued. "When I awoke, we were somewhere I didn't recognize. To make a long story short, I waited for the right opportunity and managed to escape. I made sure I wasn't followed, but every time I close my eyes, I see them. The dark mages. Their powers are unlike any I've ever seen."

Yuki placed a hand on Penny's shoulder, but Penny flinched. Yuki frowned and pulled her hand back, wanting to give Penny more space.

Yuki cleared her throat. "You're safe now. We're here."

"And we won't let you out of our sight." There was a slight quiver in Loni's voice.

"What happened to your hand?" Jae asked. "We

haven't had a doctor out here yet, but if you need medical attention—"

"No. I took care of it." Penny shook her head. "I mean, it hurts, but it will heal. What about you?" Penny asked. "What did I miss while I was… away? Are the daggers safe?"

"Yes," Darshana answered. "We've taken a page out of the Sacred Keys' book and decided to hide them individually."

"Oh?" Penny's brows squished together.

"Instead of them all being in one place for the Pishacha to find," Mr. Kitaro began, "we spread them out. Each one hidden by an elite mage, and each location kept a secret."

Penny handed her empty teacup to Yuki. "So, none of you knows where the others have hidden theirs?"

"No." Salina let out a breath. "And hopefully the Pishacha won't come close to discovering any of the locations."

"Wait." Penny furrowed her brow. "You said the elites hid them, but there were only six of you until I showed up. What about the seventh dagger?"

"I took it upon myself to hide that one," Mr. Kitaro said. "It felt in keeping with my original duty to protect the dagger."

Penny nodded slowly, taking in the news. "And what about the grimoire?"

Mayhara and Jae exchanged looks.

"Well, we found the grimoire and lost it in the same day." Jae raked a hand through his hair as he scoffed. "Practically in the same hour. We had to battle with a couple of those dark mages. But the good news is—"

"She's waking up!"

They all turned at the sound of Shiro's voice. He hovered over Karina, who let out a small moan as she shifted on the couch. Karina's small form shifted slightly, the pallor of her skin paler than usual. Her dark, unkempt hair fanned out on the sides of her face. It wasn't until Karina opened her eyes and sat up that Mayhara could release the breath she'd been holding. She sent a silent thankful prayer up to the gods that everyone in their group seemed to be all right. At least for the moment.

Three

Bhutano closed the bathroom door and locked it. Now that he was alone, he could finally let down his guard. He turned to the mirror and slowly ran a hand down the face of the body he was inhabiting. The girl's skin was smooth and soft, her eyes intense with small specks of purple.

They'd bought it. They believed he was Penny, the elite amethyst mage.

He'd reached her in time, the night of the attack. He'd felt his spirit leaving the police chief's body, and he'd only had a matter of seconds before his hold on the police chief's essence would unravel and Bhutano's spirit would be sucked into the parallel realm. But he'd successfully transcended from the chief of police's dying body into full-of-life Penny. And the plan was to go to the other elites to find out where the daggers were—without the elites being tipped off about who he really was.

So far, so good.

Possessing the body of an elite mage was an entirely new feeling to him—even as an ancient spirit who was the right hand to the greatest deity in the universe.

Penny's magic coursed through her veins, and Bhutano felt every flutter, every vibration, the warm core of it pulsing inside. Her powers of insight allowed him to understand her journey, how she'd acquired the daggers in the first place, and how close she'd become to the other elites. He knew her story, how she was an orphan, and how she now considered the elite mages her family.

He knew all this, and most importantly, he knew he could use Penny's magic when he needed to.

Bhutano took the Linq out of his hidden pocket and pressed the button to call Naree. Leaning closer to the door, he listened to make sure no one was in the hall to hear him. Though he would still sound like Penny, he didn't want the elite mages to hear what he was discussing. Talking to anyone on the phone would be suspicious enough.

"Hello?" Naree sounded hesitant.

"It's me," Bhutano said. "I'm in."

For a moment, Naree didn't respond. Bhutano figured she was still unsure that it was truly him.

"They believe you're her?" Naree asked.

"Yes. There's no reason for them to doubt it."

It was the same as when he'd possessed the body of the Imperial Police chief. No one had suspected he'd really been the spirit messenger—except, of course, those who'd been in on the entire operation, those who were followers of Kashmeru and his cause.

"Did you find the daggers?" Naree asked.

"It's more complicated than we believed," Bhutano

explained. "The elite mages have hidden the daggers separately and have kept the locations of each a secret from each other."

Again, Naree was quiet, no doubt contemplating this new problem. "Should we come in with the dark mages? Force them to disclose the hiding places?"

"With the daggers spread out as they are, it would be difficult to do. I can't see that plan being a hundred percent successful. But I have another idea."

"What is it?"

"They believe I'm their friend. I can get them to open up to me."

"But if they're keeping the locations a secret from each other—"

"I'm not going to ask them where the daggers are. I suspect they won't tell me." Bhutano grinned to himself. "I'm going to lower their defenses, and then I'm going to use our dear amethyst mage's powers of insight to search their minds and show me where the daggers are. Without them even knowing it."

"Do you think you can manage it?" Naree asked. "You don't exactly have much experience using her powers."

"It worked enough to find this dismal place they're holed up in. I have confidence I can figure it out." Bhutano took another look in the mirror, moving Penny's dark waves away from her cheeks. "I learned something else."

Naree sighed into the Linq. "Something good or bad?"

"That depends. The guru says the approach of the comet is affecting the mages' powers."

"Affecting them how?"

"Apparently, it's causing some kind of disruption. Their powers aren't working to full capacity. Have the dark mages reported anything of that nature?"

"Not that I know of, but I'll talk with them and let you know for certain."

"Good. How are things going with the grimoire?"

"Tien Thi is studying it. She says some of the language is ancient, words witches nowadays don't tend to use anymore. But she believes she understands enough to find the correct spell to unlock Kashmeru from his tomb."

"Good." Bhutano just hoped their witch was powerful enough to do the spell once she found it. "If not, I may have another plan. There's a witch here they seem to hold in high regards. I'll do some digging and find out if her level of power exceeds that of Tien Thi. If that's the case, then we can use her instead. But we'll have to wait to grab her until after we've acquired all the daggers."

"It seems to all be falling into place."

Bhutano smiled. "Yes. It does. I need to go before they get suspicious. But I'll report back with what I can find out. We can send dark mages in bit by bit when I discover a location. That way, we can steal the daggers back one by one, right from under their noses."

Penny was screaming. But no one could hear her. She wondered if Bhutano had somehow muted her voice in the space he occupied in her head. She could see everything he saw, hear everything he said, and witness everything he did. But she was powerless to stop him. She heard his plan to trick the other mages into revealing where they'd hidden the daggers, but she could do nothing to warn them.

There was no way to control Bhutano's movements as he moved her body into the dining room to join the others.

"Are you sure you don't need to lie down for a while?" Salina asked.

Salina, it's not me. It's Bhutano. Please. He's lying to you.

"I can lie down later," Bhutano said with Penny's voice. "I'm actually starving."

Salina smiled and pulled out Penny's chair for her.

"How's Karina?" Jae asked Shiro as he placed a large serving plate of stir-fried noodles on the table.

Jae, please! Bhutano's got you fooled!

"She's getting some rest," Shiro replied. "She apologized for not joining us. I think she's trying to get used to the power transfer."

"Power transfer?" Bhutano asked in Penny's body.

Everyone looked at Penny.

"We won't know if it worked for sure until she tests it," Darshana said, taking a seat at the head of the table. "But I think we should give her time to mourn. It can't be easy to concentrate when you've just buried your grandmother."

Bhutano shifted in the chair. "I'd like to offer my condolences to her later. When she's up for it. I still can't believe Amalia's gone."

Penny wanted to grit her teeth and pound her fist against the table, but she couldn't do either. Bhutano hadn't even known Amalia, and he was pretending to grieve her passing, all as a ruse to find out if Karina was powerful enough to unlock Kashmeru's tomb.

"It's a bittersweet day," Mr. Kitaro said with a nod. "We've said our goodbyes to Amalia, but we are also grateful to have Penny back."

The elite mages followed Mr. Kitaro's lead and raised their glasses.

"Welcome back," Darshana said.

Penny could not stop Bhutano from raising his glass in return. If she could, she would have thrown the glass and shouted to them all that they were being duped.

Help me, Darshana. Hear me!

Four

Karina ran her fingers along the length of the small scroll, feeling the tiny bumps in the golden clasp on the side. Was it a code? Or simply imperfections? She couldn't be sure. All she knew was they'd had the scroll for over a week now and still had no idea how to open it. It was about half the diameter of the other scrolls they'd been dealing with, and three-quarters the length. It appeared to be sealed by the golden clasp, but none of them could pry it open. They had tried for days when Jae and Mayhara had brought it back from the Bhaja Caves, but then they'd had to organize Amalia's funeral, and thoughts of the scroll had had to wait.

With a sigh, she went to the window. The sky was cloaked in a pinkish orange hue by the horizon. She was struck with a memory from her childhood, when she'd been at the swamp with her grandmother. Amalia had been teaching her about which herbs to use in a certain potion, and the sun had begun to set. Amalia had stopped, mid-speech, and smiled at the sky.

"What is it, Grandmother?" Karina had asked.

Amalia had gazed down at her, giving her a sideways grin. "Did you know that when you were very small, you had lighter hair?"

Karina had giggled. "Strawberry blonde, right?"

"It was an odd thing," Amalia had remarked. "But a few of our ancestors have been blessed with the feature when they were small as well. They'd all grown out of it, of course. But they were all—each of them—also blessed with being very special witches with extraordinary purposes."

"You think I'm special too?"

Amalia had stroked her cheek. "Indeed."

Karina had screwed up her face and looked at the sky. "But why are you smiling at the sky, Grandmother?"

"Because, truly, your hair was more the color of the sky right now at the horizon than a strawberry blonde."

Karina blinked away the memory, focusing again on the tinged horizon. Was she a special witch with an extraordinary purpose? She knew her grandmother had to be right. And taking in her current situation, helping the elite mages in their attempt to save the world, she believed it must be her fate.

So what was missing? Why couldn't she open the scroll? It had crossed her mind, more than once, that the answer might lie in the grimoire that had been stolen away at the most inopportune moment.

She let out a grunt and held the scroll to her forehead.

"Come on," she said to herself.

She had to try again. Grimoire or not. Her brain scrambled for a spell she hadn't tried yet. For what seemed like forever, she paced her room, searching the recesses of her mind for a spell that would work.

Setting down the scroll, she gathered a few of her grandmother's candles and placed them on the floor. After she lit them, she sat cross-legged in front of the flickering flames and placed the scroll on her leg. It was so small, that, if not for the length of it, she could hide it in a closed fist. The golden clasp reflected the flames, and Karina felt hypnotized by the changing lights.

She closed her eyes and waited for the spell to come to her. Sounds became louder in her ears. She let them in and listened for a message. Between the sound of the wind outside, the call of birds, the buzzing of insects, and the muffled movements of the others in the house, a low whisper reached her ears.

At first, Karina felt a jolt, like a tremor of fear exploding in her head. She forced herself to stay her ground and keep listening. The murmur grew louder. Was it her grandmother's voice? Her heart pounded, and she listened harder.

"…deceiving you!"

Karina's mouth hung open. She started shaking. But

she didn't want to break the connection. "Grandmother?"

She listened more closely, trying to tell if it was her grandmother's voice or not. It was still too staticky to tell for sure. The murmur echoed, as if it were being spoken through a tunnel. *"…deceiving…"*

A ringing began in her ears. She tried to keep listening to the voice, but the ringing grew louder. An ache blossomed in her neck. Her shoulders scrunched up, and she gritted her teeth. The ringing became unbearable, until she had no choice but to cover her ears and scream for it to stop.

The candles went out all at once, and Karina's breaths were heavy. But the ringing had stopped.

The door to her room was thrown open, and Karina looked up to see Salina standing there.

"Are you all right?" Salina scanned the room. "I heard a scream."

Karina scrubbed her hands down her face. "Sorry. It's okay. I'm fine."

Salina took a few steps into the room. "What happened?"

Karina sighed. "I was trying to figure out how to open

the scroll, and then…"

"And then what?"

Karina bit her lip. "It's going to sound crazy."

"With everything we've been through in the past month, *crazy* might actually be normal."

"Okay." Karina grimaced. "While I was trying to listen to the voice in my head to figure out the right spell to use on the scroll, I thought I heard my grandmother's voice."

Salina offered her a small smile. "That's not crazy; that's normal. When my mom passed away, I swore I heard her calling my name a hundred times in about as many days. I think it's the heart's way of holding on to the loved ones we've lost. I still hear Huojin's voice on occasion."

"You do?"

"Yeah. She hasn't been gone that long." Salina frowned.

"That's true. And you've hardly had time to grieve." Karina sighed once more. "I guess it's just something I need to get used to. For now."

"I guess. It'll get better. And if you ever need anyone

to talk to, you know where to find me."

"Thanks."

Salina gave her a single nod and then turned to leave the room.

Karina picked up the scroll from the floor and ran her fingers over it again. She would keep trying. Whatever it took.

"*…deceiv—*"

Karina dropped the scroll and slapped a hand against her chest. Swallowing hard, she recalled what Salina had said. It was just her heart's way of holding on.

She forced herself to calm down. But even after her breathing slowed to normal, she had to wonder: Why would her heart be telling her that someone was deceiving her?

Five

Jae ran the program for the fifth time, leaning back in the hair at the desk in Mr. Kitaro's office. He locked his fingers behind his head as he waited for the system to run through its files. His eyes were tired from staring at the monitor, and his hope of finding Naree was slowly depleting.

Part of him wondered had he been there when Loni and Salina had found Penny, if he would have been able to convince Naree to come with him. To leave Kashmeru's grasp and join the side she was meant to be on. He'd convinced her before, when he and Mayhara had chased down Naree in the caves near Sariska. Of course, his victory had only lasted one night, and his sister had been gone in the morning. Stolen away again by Kashmeru.

Now all he had to rely on was the facial recognition software. Maybe she'd slipped up when she'd fled the villa with the Pishacha. Maybe some street camera had caught a shot of her. Then he'd have a clue where to start looking.

He needed his sister back—in her true form, not this delusional, bad-boy-obsessed version of her that fought him every step of the way. And not just because he promised his parents, but because the world depended on it.

And he was running out of time.

"The news is talking about Police Chief Min's funeral." Darshana stood in the doorway of the office. "I hope I'm not interrupting."

"Not at all." Jae leaned forward in his chair. "Are they

still claiming it was a heart attack?"

"That's their coverup story, yes."

Jae tapped a button on the keyboard. A window appeared on the screen displaying a muted news reel. Sure enough, the Imperial Police chief's photo was featured in the report.

Another figure appeared at the office door, and Jae straightened in his chair. "Karina. How are you feeling?"

Karina stepped inside the office and sat in the chair opposite Jae. She had her hair pulled back in a low ponytail, and the dark circles were gone from under her eyes. "I feel… different. I guess my body is still adjusting. I can't tell if I need to go for a run or if I'm too exhausted to move. My brain feels numb and full of a million thoughts all at once. And everything… tingles."

Darshana stepped forward and rested a hand on Karina's shoulder. "I'm afraid I can't guide you through this. Mage powers, I can help with. But witch powers are out of my skillset."

"Then I guess you won't know how I'm supposed to crack this puzzle." Karina held up the small scroll Mayhara had luckily slipped past the dark mages and the Pishacha when the grimoire had been stolen from them.

According to Karina, the scroll was said to contain a spell that could destroy Kashmeru for good. No one in the empire had known about it, and Jae suspected the Pishacha were also clueless about its existence. The only hint that the scroll existed was the vision Darshana had had of it. The scroll was small enough that Jae hadn't noticed Karina holding it when she'd first come into the room.

"It still won't open?" Jae asked.

Karina shook her head and sighed. "I'm not sure if it needs a spell to unlock it, or a secret word, or… a hammer."

Darshana let out a laugh. "I'm sure it will come to you. A witch locked it, and it will take a witch to open it."

"I just thought, with my grandmother's powers…" Karina grew silent.

Jae and Darshana exchanged a glance.

"Perhaps it can only be opened when it's needed," Darshana suggested. "Some kind of guarantee the witches who created it thought up so it wouldn't be destroyed."

"Maybe." Karina didn't seem convinced.

Jae's eyes wandered to the monitor. The image of Director Shei appeared in the newsreel window. Leaning forward, Jae clicked the button to make the window full screen and turned on the volume.

"Shei, who is in charge of the comet's arrival celebration at the Bahá'í Lotus Temple in New Delhi, has stated that plans are moving forward despite the unexpected death of Police Chief Min. She's quoted as saying that he would have wanted the celebration to continue, knowing how important welcoming the Akutake comet is to the citizens of New United Asia. The celebration coincides with the temple's grand reopening, after almost five years of extensive renovations. Astronomers say the comet's closest proximity to Earth will take place at the end of next week when it will be exactly above the temple's apex."

"That's it," Darshana said.

"What?" Jae watched as Darshana's eyes narrowed in thought.

"That's where Kashmeru must be buried."

Karina shifted in her chair to get a better look at the guru. "What makes you think that?"

"The temple has been under construction for the last five years. No one's been in there except authorities and construction crews, and as we all know, the government is tied in with the Pishacha. The comet will be closest when it reaches the sky directly above the temple—which has a star-shaped window at its top, called the symbol of the Greatest Name."

"A conveniently placed window," Jae said.

"Exactly. One should be able to see the comet's light through it," Darshana said.

"And feel its energy," Karina added.

"So, you think Kashmeru's tomb is somewhere in the temple?" Jae asked.

"My best guess is it's under the temple. But directly below that window."

Jae smirked. "I guess we'll find out."

Darshana gave him a nod in agreement. "I also wanted to talk to you about this meteor shower that's taking place later this week."

"What meteor shower?" Karina asked.

"It's not a big deal," Jae said. "We have them all the time, actually. But I think people are focusing on this one because it's taking place so close to the time of the comet's arrival."

"Yes, and it gave me an idea," Darshana said, placing her hands together.

"What is it?" Jae asked.

"So meteoroids are rock and debris that have burned off from comets that circle the sun, and the Earth occasionally crosses the orbit of these comets, causing us to traverse through the cloud of debris. And if this cloud, which we are approaching—or is approaching us, whichever way you want to see it—gets in the way of the Akutake comet, couldn't it be that it somehow disrupts the disruption?"

Jae picked up a pen and tapped it on the desktop. "You mean lessen the effect of the comet?"

"Precisely." Darshana raised a brow and waited for him to answer.

"Perhaps." He clicked away on the computer keyboard. "Let's put it on our schedule. We could go to the nearest hill, whichever is the highest point, and test out your theory.”

Darshana gave him a wink. “Smart boy. That's what I thought you'd say.”

Six

Shiro concentrated on his fingers as he pushed out his magic. Like a leaky faucet, small drops of water pooled at the fingertips and slowly dripped, one by one, to the ground. He made a fist and looked up at the blue sky, gritting his teeth in frustration. Closing his eyes, he called upon Darshana's breathing technique.

Breathe in for four seconds. Hold for seven. Calmly exhale for eight.

He could sense the heavy weight lift from his shoulders and a warmth radiating throughout his body. Feeling calmer, he opened his eyes and took in his surroundings.

The meadow was peaceful. He could hear the babbling of the nearby stream, and the call of white-cheeked barbets echoed around him. He breathed in and out again. This time, when he extended his hand and pushed out his powers, pellets of ice shot out and zoomed into a nearby tree. The birds in that tree took off, frightened by the sudden impact.

The release of energy was exhilarating. Still, he worried his lip with his teeth. This interference of power the comet was causing was bad news. In the heat of battle against the Pishacha, there would be no time for breathing exercises. The elite mages needed to be at their best when the time came. Their powers needed to be fully loaded and ready to go.

"That's good, isn't it?"

Shiro turned to see Penny standing in a patch of

flowers nearby. Her head was tilted, her hands clasped behind her back, and her smile was small.

"Yeah." He rubbed the back of his head and gestured to the tree pocked with ice. "It's not my best work, but at least I'm able to get my powers to work at all."

Penny came closer. "It's strange, this unexpected effect of the comet."

"I'm worried about how much worse it might get."

The buzz of Shiro's Linq interrupted his train of thought. When he spotted Qiang's name on the screen, his heart skipped a beat.

He glanced at Penny and held a finger up before answering the call. "Qiang?"

"Shiro, I'm in Guwahati. And it looks bad."

"What happened?" Shiro's eyes went to Penny, who gave him a questioning look.

"Every mage I've managed to come into contact with inside the camps—their powers have been stripped."

Shiro rubbed the crease in his forehead, letting out a curse. "It's the comet. It's affecting their powers."

"I'm not so sure," Qiang said. "I've seen the effect with my own team. Timing is off, force is weakened, but the powers are still there. These mages in the camps, they have nothing left. It's like their power has been drained entirely. All of them. All at the same time."

Shiro blinked in confusion as he processed Qiang's words. "Any trace of explosives? Jae said the police chief and Director Shei mentioned blowing up the camps."

"If there are any here, they're well hidden. We didn't exactly walk in the front door and ask for a tour. We had to sneak in just to speak to the prisoners. Mitty and Bao checked where they could but didn't find anything suspicious. And I don't even want to get into the diversion we had to create just to get back out of the camps again."

Though he knew Qiang couldn't see him, he nodded. "Thank you, Qiang."

"We'll head to Jabalpur next and see what we can find there." Qiang let out a breath. "I heard the chief of police died."

"He is dead," Shiro responded. "But the media and the government are covering up how he died."

"Why would they do that?"

"Because he was killed by an elite mage. And because it wasn't really him at the time."

"I'm not sure I know what you mean."

Shiro glanced at Penny once more, not sure if his words would serve as a trigger for what she'd gone through at the villa. "Min was possessed by Bhutano, Kashmeru's spirit messenger. His death occurred in a fight with two of our elites."

Qiang was quiet for a moment. "Do you think Bhutano died with him? Or do you think his spirit left Min's body?"

"I can't be sure of anything."

There was noise in the background. Shiro heard Qiang's muffled voice and waited for him to speak again.

"I need to go. There are too many Imperial Police in the vicinity. We're about to leave for Jabalpur."

"Okay. Qiang?"

"Yes?"

"Be careful."

"I will."

Shiro tucked his Linq away and let out a shuddered breath.

"What was that about?" Penny asked, coming closer.

"Qiang and his team are checking out the prison

camps. He said all the mages there lost their powers."

Penny gawked at him for a moment before wrapping her arms around herself. "That's terrible."

Shiro rested his hands on his sides and dropped his head in thought. Penny put a hand on his shoulder.

"You're worried about him," she said.

"Yeah. I mean, that's Qiang. He's always thrown caution to the wind. But the thought of him getting caught—of getting hurt or killed—I don't think my heart could bear it."

"Tell me about him." Penny offered him a small smile. "How did you meet?"

The prisoners were given chores inside the camps. Shiro was assigned to the agricultural team, and the guards placed them all—probably close to a hundred mages—in one large bunker together, filled with bunk beds and thin, itchy blankets. Shiro's duties were comprised of plowing a field with a small handheld shovel, since the prisoners weren't to be trusted with tools that could double as a weapon. The fact that the shovel was dull and constructed of a light wood made Shiro's task that much harder.

The guards enjoyed hovering while the prisoners worked. The sun was especially cruel, and there were no protective hats provided for anyone other than the guards. Shiro was covered in dirt and only stopped digging for a moment to wipe the sweat from his eyes.

"No slacking, inmate!"

Something hard hit Shiro in the back, causing him to fall forward into the dirt.

Holding back a grunt, he pushed himself up to his knees. Glancing to his left, he spotted the nearest fellow prisoner. The young man looked to be his age, his black hair slicked to his forehead with sweat. His kind eyes seemed to reach out to Shiro, to tell him to hang in there.

Shiro gave him the smallest of nods and then shoved his shovel into the dirt again to continue his work.

The guard paced behind him, no doubt scanning the others to make sure they were doing their jobs. Risking a glance over his shoulder, Shiro noticed the weapon the guard carried. The one he'd used to hit him in the back. It was the same weapon the Imperial Police had used when they'd attacked the academy. Cyber batons, he'd heard one of the other mages call them. They were something new the Imperial Police were armed with to use against mages in case the blocking devices in the mages' necks didn't stop them from using their powers.

The guard whipped his head around and caught Shiro gawking. Baring his teeth, the guard marched forward and lifted his weapon. "I said, no slacking!"

In the next second, Shiro was struck across his cheek. Electric pulses vibrated through his head in a violent tempo. The next thing he felt was his head hitting the ground. Black spots danced before his eyes as he tried to clear his double vision and right himself. Footfalls met his ears mixed with a high-pitched ringing.

"I never liked bullies," came a voice from behind him.

There was a thump and a grunt, and Shiro opened his eyes wide enough to see the guard, face-down in the dirt beside him, blood streaming from his temple.

Shiro let out a gasp and backed away from him. He turned to see the black-haired young man extending a hand.

"Come on," the young man said. "You don't belong in the mud."

Shiro took his hand and let him pull him to his feet. His heart raced, but not just because this young man had fought back against a prison camp guard.

The guard let out a moan, and Shiro swallowed hard.

"He's getting up." Shiro almost stuttered his words.

His fellow prisoner gave a nod. "Looks that way. I'm Qiang, by the way."

"Shiro."

"You might want to get out of here, Shiro."

"But he could kill you."

"He'll try."

Shiro noticed the big rock Qiang gripped in his hand. The field was mostly mud and dirt. Where had Qiang gotten the rock from? Unless…

Qiang gestured toward another prisoner about fifty meters away. "That's Mitty. Go to him. He'll take care of you."

"What about you?"

Before Qiang could answer, the guard shot up into a crouching position and swung his cyber baton, cracking Qiang across his legs. Qiang let out a shout as he buckled to his knees.

"Go, Shiro!"

Shiro was ready to ignore Qiang's instructions and jump in to help, but he spotted two more guards racing toward them.

Qiang delivered a quick fist to the guard's jaw. "Shiro! Go!"

He could feel his heartbeat pounding in his throat as he backed away from the fight. A fight he hadn't been involved in. He realized then that Qiang was trying to keep Shiro innocent in the whole ordeal so he wouldn't be punished. He swallowed hard and turned to dash toward Mitty.

It was a blur after that. And it wasn't until night fell that Shiro saw Qiang again.

Shiro was lying in bed, staring at the underside of the bunk above him, when the door to their bunker was torn *open and someone was tossed inside. A low grunt was let out by the person sprawled out on the floor, and the guards at the door delivered anyone who could see a menacing scowl before slamming the door shut again.*

Those closest to the commotion got up to inspect the situation. Shiro shot out of his bed, knowing it must have been Qiang. He pushed his way through the dozens of inmates gathered near the door to find Qiang beaten black and blue. His bare back exposed long, swollen gashes of bloody flesh where the guards must have tortured him—probably with their cyber batons. Though Qiang's condition looked terrible, Shiro was happy he was still alive.

"Move out of the way." Mitty appeared, the large mass of him, moving through the crowd and toward Qiang. He crouched down and slung one of Qiang's arms over his muscular shoulders. "Make room!"

Shiro followed them to what must have been Qiang's bed. He hissed through his teeth when he saw that one of Qiang's eyes was swollen to the size of a softball, purple and red and practically swallowing the eyeball.

"Qiang," Shiro said hesitantly.

Qiang glanced up, his one visible eye softening when he caught sight of Shiro. He gave him a nod, letting him know it was all right to come closer.

"I'll see if anyone's got any bandages," Mitty said before stepping away.

Shiro dropped down on his legs beside Qiang's bed. "I'm so sorry. This is because of me."

Qiang winced as he turned his head to face Shiro better. "No, Shiro. Don't ever blame yourself. We are the victims here. They are the bad guys. Don't ever forget that."

Shiro blinked as he nodded. "Did you… That rock that was in your hand. Did you use your powers to make it?"

Qiang searched Shiro's face. "Yes."

"But the blocker? How were you not shocked by it?"

"I was," Qiang said. "But I've built up a tolerance. One day, I'm going to get out of this place. Nothing these jackasses do can keep me here. Blockers. Torture. No matter. I will prevail. Our people don't deserve to be in *here. We did nothing wrong. And I'm going to make it right. Somehow."*

Shiro sat in wonder of Qiang's determination. He felt some small spark of hope. "Will you teach me?"

Qiang's brow furrowed. "What?"

"How to tolerate the pain. I want to help you."

The smallest hint of a smile tugged on Qiang's lips. "Yes. I will. I'll teach you."

"He sounds too good to be true," Penny said, stirring Shiro from his memories.

Shiro took in a deep breath, his mind circling for a moment—from Qiang, to the extremists, to their war against the Pishacha, to the daggers, and finally to his need to make sure he had control over his powers—before he could properly register Penny's comment.

"No. Of course not." Shiro let out a laugh. "Nobody's perfect. But I can't think of anyone more perfect for me."

Seven

"Are you near?"

Naree scanned the area, her focus landing on the quaint cabin tucked away in the distance. It was a small source of light in the landscape of night. "Yes, we're near."

"Good," Bhutano said into the Linq. "The dagger is

in the bank of the stream. I would have marked its exact location, but I was being watched. Look for the bend near the woods."

"We'll find it." Naree walked in the direction of the stream, signaling for the two dark mages who were with her—Ru and Avi—to follow. "They still don't suspect you of impersonating the elite?"

"No."

"And one of them simply let you see their thoughts? Just like that?"

"I had him tell me a story from his past. Made him focus on something emotional so his defenses regarding the dagger were stripped down enough for me to see into his mind."

"Fantastic."

"Find the dagger," Bhutano instructed. "I'll make sure no one leaves the house tonight. But keep out of sight, just in case."

He ended the call, and Naree slipped her Linq into her pocket.

They trudged through the untended fields, over rocky terrain and patches of mud. Once they reached the stream, it didn't take them long to find the spot Bhutano had mentioned. Naree reached out with her crimson powers to feel the earth and sand at the stream's bend, tuning in on where the dagger was hidden.

"It's in the water. Here," she said to the dark mages at her side. "Buried under some heavy rocks."

"Want me to go in?" Avi asked.

"One moment." Naree extended her hands, the orange glow of her copper powers emanating in the palm of each. As if the world were tipping on its side, water moved away from the edge of the stream, moved as if a wall were being created to keep it away, exposing the slick earth and pebbles of the bank. She kept her arms extended and gave Avi a nod. "Now."

Avi scrutinized the exposed riverbank and jumped into the area that was free from water. His shoes partly sunk into the squishy bottom. He glanced behind him as if checking that the stream was being held back by Naree's invisible, magical dam. Crouching down, Avi moved his fingers around, digging them into the mud and feeling the rocks embedded in the sides of the riverbed.

"Let me help," Ru said, reaching out with her powers.

One by one, the bigger rocks lifted from the mud, breaking free with a sucking and popping sound.

"I see it." Avi reached into the muck and pried free the metal object. He stood and wiped the blade, smiling at the way the moonlight reflected off it.

"Get out of there," Ru urged, motioning for him to hurry. "We still have to leave the property before anyone sees us."

The moment he cleared the riverbed, Naree released her powers. The water rushed back in place, splashing against the bank.

"We got it," Avi said, his eyes twinkling.

Naree threw her hair back from her shoulders, but she didn't smile. There was still much more to do, and they'd only just started. Still, they were headed in the right direction.

She gave him a curt nod. "Yes. We got it."

Naree slunk down into the hot water, bubbles rising and

covering her skin. She breathed in the steam and closed her eyes, resting the back of her head against the cool edge of the tub. It was a smaller tub than the one at the villa, but it did the trick just as well. Though the villa had been comfortable and luxuriously pleasing, the penthouse apartment they'd gone to after escaping was just as cozy, even if it was only a portion of the size. Plus, it had a breathtaking view of the New Sudamapur city skyline.

She had to admit, the change of location was not as jarring as the change in Bhutano's host. When the police chief had collapsed before her eyes, she hadn't been sure Bhutano's spirit had transferred at all. It wasn't until the eyes of the amethyst mage had opened and she'd spoken that Naree could accept what had happened. It was strange listening to Bhutano's messages being said in Penny's voice, but once he'd laid out his plan for her and the dark mages, she had no doubt that it was really him.

She glanced over at the sink. Next to it, on the counter, lay the dagger. After bringing it back from the river, she'd washed it off and set it on the counter to dry, and then decided her body could use a good soaking as well.

You've done well, my love.

She ran her fingertips along her soapy skin and grinned at Kashmeru's words.

You're proving your worth.

"The comet's getting closer," she said. "It's almost time."

We'll soon be together and rule over our own new realm.

"Rule… together?" She was filled with a tingling warmth that brought tears to her eyes.

Yes, my love. We are so close.

Eight

Salina clutched the hairpin in her hand, staring into her cup of tea as she sat alone in the kitchen. The pin's sharp edge pinched the skin of her palm, but she didn't loosen her grip. The pain reminded her of the loss she hadn't had the proper time to mourn.

"Why are you sitting alone in the dark?"

Salina looked up to find Penny approaching the table from out of the shadows.

"The kettle's still hot if you'd like to join me," Salina said.

"Sounds perfect." Penny fetched a cup from the cupboard and picked out tea leaves from a canister. "Can't you sleep?"

Salina sighed. "I guess you could say silent ghosts are keeping me up."

"Ghosts?"

Salina opened her hand and placed the hairpin on the table. "Huojin. This was her hairpin. I found it within my things as I was getting ready for bed. It was just… there."

"You don't remember bringing it with you?" Penny watched her as she sipped her tea.

"Maybe absentmindedly. But tonight… I don't know. It was like it was speaking to me. Telling me to remember Huojin. To hang in there and fight this fight for her. Like she'd want me to."

"She meant a lot to you." It was more of a statement than a question.

"She was my best friend." Salina ran her fingers over

the golden grooves of the pin.

"I don't really remember her that well," Penny said. "From our academy days. Tell me about how you became friends."

Salina shifted in her chair, a small smile forming on her lips. "Well, we were both in Golden House…"

Salina lowered her hand. She'd hit the target, just as her guru had instructed, but she couldn't help but compare her skills to her classmates. Was her fire not as bright as theirs? Slower somehow? She could have sworn a couple of the other golden mages had snickered when she'd taken her stance during her turn.

Her stomach roiled, but she refused to drop her head. After all, she wouldn't have been admitted to the academy if her skills weren't up to par.

"All right, class," their guru called. "That's all for today. Make sure you practice your small flames for next week's precision exam."

As they began to clear out of the training area, three of her classmates approached her.

"You're the new girl, right?" the only male of the three asked. He had light brown hair that stuck up in all directions. Salina suspected he was trying to make it look like fire.

"Yeah," Salina answered. She forced herself to stand tall, like her mother always told her to do. "Two weeks now."

The boy held out his hand. "I'm Ken."

"Yes, I know." Salina offered a small smile as she shook his hand. "You're the golden elite."

"You've been paying attention," Ken said with a smirk.

"I'm Salina."

"This is Lin and Cora." He tilted his head to each side to gesture toward them.

Lin and Cora, whom Salina realized were twins, gave Salina a half-nod mixed with a half-bow, which Salina returned.

"A bunch of us were going to meet up at the cemetery for a party tonight." Ken looked her up and down. "You up for it?"

"Um. The cemetery?" Salina crossed her arms. "Isn't that off-campus?"

Lin shrugged "And?"

"I thought we're not allowed off-campus after curfew."

"You got a problem with breaking curfew?" Cora raised a brow.

Salina was about to pass on the invitation, but part of her was flattered that the golden elite and his friends were inviting her to a party. To include her in their group. Maybe even to call her one of their own.

"No, no problem." Salina waved a dismissive hand, deciding to give in to temptation. "I'll see you there."

"Great." Ken flashed a smile with his perfect teeth.

They parted ways, and Salina gathered her things to head back to her dorm.

She was filled with an excitement that made her tremble. She'd been so nervous coming to New United Asia without her family. Not a minute went by in which she hadn't longed to linq home and hear her parents' voices. She didn't want to dwell on how much she felt *alone, but in the two weeks since she'd been at the Empire of the Lotus Academy, every day she faced made her feel like an outsider.*

But now she had the opportunity to be part of something, to shed her outsider persona and actually feel like she belonged.

She hadn't brought much with her from Eritrea, but her mother had given her a couple of nice outfits for special occasions. She opted not to wear the dress. It seemed like a cemetery-party fashion faux pas. Picking out a vibrant blouse and a snug pair of black jeans, she set out to fix her hair and apply a little makeup. Using her golden mage powers, she carefully heated the tip of her kajal eyeliner and emphasized her golden-flecked brown eyes.

Her heart beating quickly, she checked out the final result in the mirror. She had to admit she looked like she could fit in with the popular kids. All she needed to do was slip on her boots, and she'd be ready to go.

She took long, deep breaths as she stepped out into the hallway. Glancing down the hall, she caught two girls from her house watching her and whispering. She ignored their giggles, forcing herself to walk past them. Who did they think they were anyway? She'd made new friends, and they were popular—one of them was the golden elite! Soon she would be the one laughing. She'd show them.

As she turned toward the stairwell, a hand suddenly wrapped around her arm. She turned in surprise to find a girl with big, dark eyes and silky, shoulder-length, black hair with bright pink streaks. There was no smile on her face, and for a second, Salina was worried about what the girl might say to her.

"Don't do it," the girl said.

"What?"

"The cemetery. It's a setup."

Salina narrowed her eyes. "What do you mean?"

"Ken and his lackeys. They like to prank the new kids. Get them in trouble by making them break curfew. You wouldn't be the first to fall for it."

"What?" Salina shook her head. "Why would they do that?"

"I guess some kids get bored."

Salina scoffed. "Playing with fire isn't enough for them?"

The girl let out a small laugh. "Right? I'm Huojin, by the way."

"I'm Salina."

"Nice to meet you." Huojin gave her a sideways look. "So listen. It's no party in the cemetery, but do you want to come hang out with me and my sister? Our parents just sent a care package, and I swear we've got, like, a million packs of chocolate-coated biscuit sticks, if you like those."

"I love those! Sure."

Huojin smiled and hooked her arm through Salina's. "Great."

"So you became fast friends after that?" Penny asked.

Salina's mind wandered for a moment as she was stirred from the memory. Thoughts of Huojin led to a reminder of their mission, their fight with the enemy, and the daggers. She blinked as she processed Penny's question.

"She basically took me under her wing. I was far from home, far from family, and Huojin made it a lot easier to adapt."

"Whatever happened to Ken and his gang?"

"They got busted for tricking another newbie. Detention for weeks." Salina let out a laugh. "I was always grateful to Huojin for saving me. Not just from detention—though that would have been a terrible way to begin my studies, with that black mark on my academy records. But I was grateful that she took me in and showed me there are still decent people in the world."

"Yes." Penny sipped her tea before she continued. "There certainly are those who will fall on either side of the blade of decency. It's good to know on which side the people in our lives fall."

Nine

Penny wasn't sure how much more of this she could take. Every fake conversation Bhutano was forcing her to make, every manipulative act he made her do, felt as if it were damaging her heart.

She sat at the dining room table, joining the others for dinner, but it wasn't her who controlled her movements.

As Bhutano made her look around and greet her allies, Penny was begging for someone to realize it wasn't really her.

Please. Somebody. You have to see it's an imposter. It's not me!

"Karina, how are you?" Mayhara asked.

Bhutano followed Mayhara's line of vision and Penny watched Karina approach the table.

Karina! Please. There must be something in your witch magic that makes it possible to hear me.

"I'm doing better," Karina said. "Thank you."

"This looks delicious, Mr. Kitaro," Salina said, serving herself a bowl of Agedashi tofu in black pepper broth.

"I can't take all the credit." Mr. Kitaro gave Shiro a wink. "Shiro made the green tea rice."

"It all smells amazing." Salina gave Shiro a nod.

Salina! Your dagger is not safe. Bhutano has told Naree where it is. They're going after it as we speak!

"Save some for me," Bhutano said with Penny's voice, adding a convincing laugh as he took the serving spoon from Salina.

Please. You're all in danger. They've already got

Shiro's dagger. Somebody, please hear me!

Her frustration built up inside her. She felt as if she were going to explode. She needed to take control of her body back.

In that moment, Bhutano knocked a fork off the table. Penny gasped internally. She had done that. She'd been trying to grab the reins and take control, and in some miniscule moment, she'd been able to move her own hand.

"Sorry about that," Bhutano said in her voice. "I guess I'm a little clumsy tonight."

It's possible, she said to herself. *I don't know how, but it's possible.*

But try as she might, she couldn't manage to do it again. She knew Bhutano was aware of what she was doing and was fighting against her. She had to find another moment where he was more vulnerable to her persuasion.

I won't give up. I need to keep trying.

Ten

The small church sat high on a hill, the cherry blossom trees surrounding it littered with falling petals. It was almost noon, and the place was practically empty.

Naree climbed the stone steps to the building's open double doors. Peering inside, she gave a nod, signaling for

Avi and Ru to follow. She removed her sunglasses and pushed back the scarf covering her hair, scanning the rows of pews and the altar. A handful of people in prayer were spread out throughout the building. The altar was vacant, the lights above it out.

Naree moved silently through the church, both to remain unnoticed and also to not disturb the praying patrons. The dark mages followed, their footsteps undetectable to Naree's ears. They made their way past the altar and turned down a passage that led to a set of stairs.

The stairwell led downward, and only a single wall sconce lit the way. Reaching the bottom of the stairs, Naree found herself in a dark chamber. The only beacon of light in the dismal room was from a long, wooden votive candle stand upon which sat rows and rows of small red candles. Each row was elevated behind the first. Only about two dozen of what must have been over a hundred candles were lit here and there, but in the rear row, in the center, were a cluster of seven lit candles. Their flames seemed higher and brighter than the others.

"This is it," Naree said.

"How do you know?" Ru asked.

Naree reached for the candles. "It's exactly how Bhutano described it from the golden elite's mind."

As her hands got closer to move the candles, the flames grew hotter and more intense. She narrowed her eyes and withdrew her hands. "Hmm."

"What is it?" Avi asked.

"Bhutano said they have a witch working with them."

"The witch Kun poisoned?" Ru scoffed. "I'm surprised she's still alive."

"No. It's another witch," Naree replied. "Her granddaughter. I think she helped the golden elite hide this dagger. There seems to be some kind of spell to protect the hiding place with fire."

Avi studied the votive shelf. "You sure you can't just blow them out?"

"No." Naree didn't look at him as she shook her head. "That won't work. But it's fine. I'm known to have powers of my own that might help."

She raised her hands, her palms glowing a bright gold. Concentrating on pulling the fire away, she moved closer, inch by inch. The flames stretched from their wicks to her palms, flickering as her powers sucked away the heat. As the last of the flames disappeared into a tendril of smoke, Ru and Avi reached for the candles and moved them off the shelf.

"There's a latch," Avi said.

Naree bent closer and pulled on the latch, which opened a hidden compartment. The corners of her mouth tugged upward. They'd found another dagger. Her heart sped up, and there was a slight tremble in her hands as she removed it from its hiding place.

Bhutano's plan was actually working.

Eleven

Mayhara wandered into Mr. Kitaro's office to find Jae studying something on the screen. Jae glanced up as she continued toward the desk. Her eyes flit around the monitor, narrowing as she tried to figure out what he was working out. He could tell she'd recently showered; the smell of her jasmine shampoo wafted around him like a gentle caress. He forced himself not to think about it.

"It's the Baha'i Lotus Temple," he said before she had a chance to ask. "A blueprint of it, anyway. And an old one—before they started renovating it."

Her focus moved from the screen to Jae's face. For a moment, their eyes locked, and Jae felt his pulse quicken. His hopes for a reconciliation elevated when she didn't back off right away. He took a deep breath—a delicious whiff of jasmine scent along with it—and in his mind, he would be perfectly satisfied if the moment were to last beyond minutes, hours, or even days. When she finally took a step back, he released the breath but kept his eyes poised on her.

"What's the plan?" she asked as she settled in the chair across from him.

"I'm preparing for a worst-case scenario."

"Oh? Has it come to that?"

Before he could answer, two more figures appeared at the door. Jae shifted in his chair as Yuki and Loni entered the office. There was a split second of a warning look to Jae from Yuki when she caught sight of Mayhara sitting across from him. He read her expression loud and clear: *Be careful what you say.* She'd already warned Jae about Loni's vulnerable state. Loni had made her feelings for Jae clear, so finding him with Mayhara was sure to stir up jealousy in her. And with Loni's drug addiction looming in the background, Jae only hoped that Yuki's diamond mage powers were keeping Loni grounded.

"What's going on?" Yuki asked. "I feel like we're waiting for the other shoe to drop."

Mayhara gestured to Jae. "Jae was just about to reveal his big, worst-case scenario plan."

"Well," Loni said, leaning back against a cabinet. "Let's hear it."

Jae turned the monitor so they all could see. "Well, it's not a solid plan yet."

"We're all here to help," Mayhara put in.

"What is that?" Loni asked, narrowing her eyes at the screen.

Yuki took a step closer. "Looks like the Lotus temple in New Delhi."

Mayhara and Loni gave her a bemused look.

Yuki shrugged. "I had to do a paper on it, back at the

academy. I wish I could have seen it before it closed for renovations."

"What's happening at the temple?" Loni leaned forward to get a better look. "Aside from the comet welcoming ceremony. What are they calling that again?"

"The Akutake Festival." Jae rubbed one of his brows. "Darshana believes Kashmeru is buried in the temple."

"What?" Yuki's forehead scrunched up. "Where exactly?"

"Where *exactly*, we're not sure," Jae replied.

"Well, he's said to be in a tomb." Mayhara gave her earlobe a scratch. "Are there sublevels to the building?"

"Yes." Jae clicked around on windows on the screen. "But I can't find anything that might resemble an area that could contain a tomb."

"Hidden, then." Yuki stuck her hands in her pockets. "Somewhere not apparent on the blueprints."

"So, what do you mean by 'worst-case?'" Loni asked. "I'm a little confused."

Jae stretched his neck out, uncomfortable with the theory he was about to explain. "Darshana and I were wondering if it were possible for the Pishacha to have figured out a way to release Kashmeru from his tomb without the daggers."

"No." Mayhara slowly shook her head. "It's not possible. The legend says so. The blood of the Lotus."

"But it doesn't say anything in particular regarding the daggers." Jae scoffed. "We didn't even know about them until the Sacred Keys started getting killed. The Pishacha have the grimoire with the spell to unlock the tomb. They have my si—They have the Lotus. Acquiring her blood could still be accomplished without the daggers, speaking practically."

"Practicality has nothing to do with it," Loni said. "This is legend and magic we're dealing with. Why did they go through all the trouble of hunting down the daggers if they didn't need them?"

Jae rubbed at the space between his nose and his upper lip. "I asked myself the same questions. But… But let's say they do it. Somehow. Let's say they find a way. What do we do?"

"We'll need to stop them," Yuki replied. She glanced once more at the blueprints on the screen. "So we're planning an ambush."

"The small scroll." Mayhara's voice was soft, as if she were still thinking it over. "We need to get it open so we can use the spell to destroy Kashmeru if they manage to set him free."

"No." Loni shook her head. "Why are we waiting? Why don't we attack now? Destroy the tomb with Kashmeru inside before the Pishacha get a chance to release him. Strike before the comet takes away all our powers."

"No." Mayhara didn't look at Loni. Instead, her eyes were far away, obviously playing out the scenario in her head. "I don't think that will work. We won't be able to get in. That place is going to be locked up tight until the night of the festival."

"We could figure out how to get in," Loni insisted.

Jae looked between the two of them and sat back in his chair. "No, Loni. Mayhara is right."

All three women stared at him, and he knew it was for different reasons. Mayhara's stare, with her slightly raised brow and parted lips, told him she was pleased that he'd agreed with her. After not taking her side in the last dispute between her and Loni, Jae was relieved that he could justifiably defend Mayhara's views.

Loni's look of shock was most definitely because he disagreed with her, and Yuki's was probably more a look of fear at how Loni might react.

"It's heavily guarded," Jae continued. "And if we're right, and they plan to release Kashmeru next week when the comet arrives, they'll have made it impossible to get to. And even if we were to miraculously find a way in, destroying his tomb doesn't mean we'd be destroying Kashmeru. I doubt it's as easy as that to kill a god."

Loni narrowed her eyes at him, her jaw squared.

Jae turned to Mayhara, who lifted her chin as if she were claiming a victory.

"But the night of the Akutake Festival," Jae continued, "the doors will be open."

Yuki crossed her arms. "It's invitation only, though. Government officials. All the higher-ups."

"It'll be catered." Jae waved a hand through the air. "That's our way in."

Loni worried her lip. "We pretend to be staff and sneak off to look for the tomb?"

"Yes." Jae gestured at the monitor. "Which is why I've

got the blueprints pulled up. Hopefully, the renovations haven't changed the layout too much. We'll make a plan now so we know where to start looking. We've got three things working in our favor: We've got all the daggers, we've got presumably the most powerful witch in New United Asia, and we've got the small scroll with the spell to destroy Kashmeru."

"I'd say the priority would be to stop them before they release him at all," Mayhara said.

"Yes." Jae splayed his fingers out on the desk. "Especially if it means his return could kill my sister."

"But the spell…" Loni's words faded. She closed her mouth tight and her face went pale.

"What about the spell?" Jae furrowed his brow.

"The one that will destroy Kashmeru." Loni visibly swallowed. "Did no one tell you? Your sister is bonded to him. If we destroy him, and she hasn't already died from the blood sacrifice, we'll most likely kill her as well."

Twelve

Ioni was avoiding Jae. After she'd dropped the news about the spell like a bomb in his lap, she couldn't look him in the eye any longer. She hated being the one to have told him about how the spell could destroy his sister, but on the other hand, he had the right to know.

But that wasn't the only reason she needed to leave the

room; every time Jae looked at Mayhara, she could practically feel his adoration for her seeping from his pores. It sickened her. It crushed her heart and created a vacuum in her chest that sucked at her very soul.

Her hands shook, and she felt she couldn't breathe. It was too hot to stay indoors. Or, at least, it felt that way. She pulled the collar of her blouse away from her skin, stretching her neck in an attempt to get more air.

Stepping onto the porch, she raked her fingers through her hair. Her body ached for a hit of Moxy. It was the only thing that could possibly ease the torment she was going through. But she was stuck in the middle of nowhere, empty-handed. Dry. She had no choice but to push through the cravings. Push through the withdrawal.

She paced, concentrating on her breathing. She told herself that each breath was taking her one step closer to getting through this episode. The acid roiling in her stomach made her cringe, but she closed her eyes and ignored the bitter taste in her mouth, as if turning off her attention to the drug's call. Shaking out her hands to rid herself of the trembling, she blew out a hard breath, begging the ache to leave her system.

"Are you all right?"

Loni opened her eyes and spun around to find Penny watching her. She cleared her throat and wrapped her arms around her middle. "Fine. I'm fine."

Penny tilted her head. "You know me better than to think I'll buy that."

Loni's head dropped. She held back the urge to sob. "I don't know if I'm going to make it through this without breaking."

"Is there anything I can do?"

"No." Loni held her palms against her cheeks. "I'm afraid it's up to me to fight my own demons."

"Did something happen?"

Loni shook her head, though it was a symbol of her frustration rather than an answer to Penny's question. "It's… Jae, mostly. I don't know why I can't get over him. What's wrong with me?"

Penny smiled. "Nothing. Magic powers or not, you're human. And your heart—I mean, when you open your heart, you open it completely. So there's no wonder you can get easily hurt."

"Yeah, it's, uh, one of those stupid emerald mage

curses, the heart thing."

Penny let out a small laugh. "I know. And I can't blame you for being hung up on him. There was a time you two were inseparable."

Loni dropped her head, her gaze lost in a memory.

Her hair was soaking wet, sticking to her face, but she didn't care. Her hand was safe and warm in Jae's, and their pursuers hadn't been able to keep up. They ducked into the back of the small abandoned delivery truck they'd been staying in the past couple of days and crept onto the old, itchy throw rug Jae had salvaged from the dumpster outside a furniture store. It wasn't the perfect place to stay—or the safest, by any means—and a funny smell lived in the floor, but it was dry and kept them hidden from the Imperial Police. Temporarily, at least.

Jae set the bag of food they'd stolen between them and smiled at Loni. "Dinner is served."

"What do you think it is?" Loni asked with a big grin.

"Smells like eggrolls."

Loni wagged her brows at him as she peeked inside the bag. "Winner, winner, eggroll dinner."

She practically tore the bag open as she grabbed an eggroll. Jae let out a laugh as he took one for himself.

"Thanks for this," she said between bites.

"I didn't do it alone."

"No, I know. But I know you don't like stealing."

He lowered his gaze and nodded. "That's true. But this was a life-or-death situation. We haven't had a bite to eat in two days."

"Still, thank you." She held her half-eaten eggroll up. "To the better half of the team."

"Oh, I wouldn't say that." He tapped the end of his eggroll against hers. "You can be pretty amazing yourself."

She blushed as his eyes traveled over her face. The blush was warm enough to make her temporarily forget about the cold, wet night outside their truck bed sanctuary. She didn't care about any of that. As long as she was with Jae, she knew she could withstand much *worse.*

"What's the saying? That which doesn't kill us...?"

Penny came closer and placed a hand on Loni's arm. "It's true, though. Especially with you. You're one of the strongest people I know."

Loni offered her a small smile. Her mind wandered for a second, scenes flashing in her head of how far she'd come, her situation now with Jae, the struggle against Kashmeru, and the need to keep the daggers away from the enemy. "It doesn't feel that way. But thanks."

Penny's words seemed to have helped the trembling subside. Maybe Loni didn't need Moxy as much as she thought she did when she had such a caring friend to lift her up when she was down.

Thirteen

The moon was hidden behind looming clouds, making the area dark and difficult to navigate. Naree approached the hidden cave Bhutano had described. No, not a cave. A tunnel. A hollowed-out passage in the small mountain. It could have served as an underpass if any vehicles found themselves in the area. But it was highly unlikely any would, because the property was hidden away in the middle of nowhere.

It was part of the land owned by the Sacred Key the elite mages were staying with. Naree couldn't see the house from where she and her two dark mage companions were standing, but she felt a pull to investigate it.

After we find the dagger, she told herself.

Rikuto and Kun—the metal manipulator and the poisoner—came up beside her as she stopped at the entrance of the tunnel. In the vacuum of the tunnel, the mountain winds whistled and hummed. Naree felt as if the tunnel were singing her an eerie welcome song. A shiver ran up and down her spine as she scanned the curves inside of the space, searching for the spot the emerald elite had hidden the dagger.

She spread out her fingers and tugged at her own emerald powers. Playing with the wind, she guided the breeze over the inside surface of the tunnel. The tone of the whistle changed at one point. Naree moved the air back and forth over the bricks at the targeted spot a few times, narrowing in on the difference in sound.

"It's there," she said.

Rikuto stepped forward and blasted the surface with dark elemental powers. The black particles he released caused the clay and bricks to crumble, breaking away from the tunnel's inner arch. There was a loud *clunk* as the dagger broke free from its spot and dropped to the ground.

"Clever," Kun said.

Naree ignored him and bent to retrieve the dagger.

We're getting closer, my love.

Naree shivered at the sound of Kashmeru's voice.

It won't be long now.

A warm sensation filled her. She stood and faced the dark mages. "Let's go."

There was almost a skip in her step as they headed back the way they had come. Something guided her closer to the house, and her heartbeat grew stronger when she realized Jae was leaning on the railing of the porch. He was a good distance away, but she could tell it was him, even in the faint glow of the porch light. Without explaining what she was doing, she wandered closer to the house but kept hidden in the shadows of the trees.

And then suddenly, she couldn't get closer.

Her brows were drawn together when her body

stopped. Something blocked her. She was unable to get past an invisible wall.

"What the—?" Rikuto pressed his body against the invisible barrier but was unsuccessful in his efforts to move past it.

"It's a protection spell," Naree said. "Probably cast to keep out those will ill intent." She held out her hands and threw every element of magic she had at the barrier, but she couldn't break through.

As the dark mages tried with their powers, Naree glanced at Jae, checking to see if he'd spotted them, but he was facing in the other direction.

"Don't," she said, placing her hands on each of the dark mage's shoulders. "Stop."

The dark mages flashed her curious looks as they dropped their hands.

"Bhutano wouldn't want us to mess up his plan." Naree gestured toward the road with her head. "We've got the dagger. Let's head back and wait for further instructions."

Rikuto and Kun nodded in agreement and joined her as they left the property.

Naree threw one last glance over her shoulder, a strange ache in her chest as she moved farther away from her brother.

Fourteen

The mages were gathered in the main room, watching the news coverage of Police Chief Min's funeral. Shiro sat beside Loni, who bit her nails as her leg bounced. Something told him her mannerism wasn't because of the funeral, but because of something else entirely. On his other side was Salina, who sat so still, he wasn't sure if she was breathing. Her hands were clasped together tightly and held between her knees. He wondered if she was thinking about Huojin and how she'd never had a funeral. Shiro shifted in his seat and looked back at the televiewer.

The newscaster droned on about the police chief's career, his accolades, and accomplishments. When she mentioned his leadership in the Eradication, Shiro wasn't the only one to squirm in his seat.

The screen showed a wide drone shot of the cemetery, slowly zooming in to the shiny coffin holding Min's body. The coffin was covered in poppies and stood above ground, ready to be mechanically lowered into the grave. It was surrounded by a large crowd of people, mostly police officers and government officials. Standing beside Min's family were Director Shei and Governor Laghari. Director Shei's silky, black hair was pulled into an impossibly perfect bun, and not a wrinkle could be seen on her form-fitting, high-collared dress. Her mouth was in the straightest of lines as she kept her eyes trained on the ground. Governor Laghari wore a suit that screamed of expensive taste. His hair was slicked back as always, and his brows were plunged downward as if in deep thought.

In the row behind them, two young faces caught Shiro's attention. Ru—the daughter of Director Shei, and Avi—the governor's son, both of whom the elite mages knew of as two of the Pishacha's secret weapons. Dark mages. Shiro almost remarked on how inappropriate it was that dark mages were attending the police chief's funeral, but then it occurred to him that everyone at the cemetery was probably on the side of the enemy. They were all in on it. All cheerleaders for the dark god.

"... that with all the preparations for the Akutake Festival, a new police chief has yet to be assigned. Governor Laghari has stated that the position will be appointed in the days following the festival."

Jae scoffed. "Because Laghari thinks Kashmeru will have risen by then, and things like the Imperial Police won't be necessary anymore."

"They'll all be part of Kashmeru's army," Shiro added. "In the new beginning. The new world."

"New worlds?" Yuki asked.

"I heard some guards talking about it when I was in the prison camp." Shiro leaned forward and set his elbows on his knees. "Kashmeru's followers believe this world we live in will end when he is released from his tomb. The Pishacha and everyone else who worships him would be delivered unto a new realm he'll have created, and everyone who is against him will perish in this world."

"Is that why this comet event at the Lotus temple is invite only?" Salina asked.

"That's precisely why." Mr. Kitaro made his way to the center of the room, his hands planted in his pockets. "This world, the universe, it will all be destroyed as punishment for his incarceration in his tomb. Plus, the centuries he had to wait for Lakshmi to give him her heart. When it is destroyed, everyone will perish. But Kashmeru, having been released from his tomb, untethered because of the blood of the Lotus, will reward his faithful followers by granting them a resurrected life in his newly created world. That includes his love, Lakshmi, who will have made the biggest sacrifice. She will be reunited with him at last, and together they will rule as sovereigns over the new era."

Mayhara shook her head. "That's… I don't even know the right words to describe it."

"Hard to swallow?" Loni put in.

"What kind of world is that supposed to be?" Yuki tucked her hair behind her ears. "Ruled by a dark god. Living under a cruel leader."

"It would be madness," Salina said, staring down at her hands.

"They're foolish to want that," Shiro added.

"And the Lotus at his side?" Salina narrowed her eyes. "What does that mean? That she would succumb to his darkness and lose her sense of right? Of light and purity?"

Jae worried his lip, undoubtedly thinking of his sister.

"It's scary to imagine," Mayhara said.

Shiro glanced around. When his gaze landed on Penny, he realized she'd been tight-lipped the whole time. Maybe she'd seen something about the future with her amethyst vision she wasn't sharing with the group. He was about to question her when Darshana gasped.

He followed her gaze to the televiewer, where chaos was breaking out. It took a second before Shiro could wrap his head around what was happening.

Near Min's coffin, a small crowd was huddled at the ground. Around them, panic ensued. Imperial Police had their weapons drawn, some of the officers running off in one direction, as if pursuing something or someone, but all of them with looks of confusion on their faces.

"I repeat, Director Shei appears to have been the target in an obvious assassination attempt. We cannot, at this time, confirm if she has been critically wounded. All we know is some sort of projectile struck Director Shei in the neck, at which point she immediately dropped to the ground and was swarmed by her concerned family, as well as by Governor Laghari and his wife. No one seems to understand how this happened. There is no word yet on the source of this attack or the motivation behind it. This was certainly a senseless and cruel assault on an already somber occasion. We are told medics have been contacted and are on the way, but judging by the lack of movement and the grim faces of those surrounding her, it may already be too late to save the director."

Shiro covered his mouth with his hand and stood to pace. He just barely made out what the others in the room were saying.

"Oh my gods!"

"It must be the extremists."

"Who would attack at a funeral?"

"Do you think she's really dead?"

Shiro's gut twisted. He knew it had to be Qiang or one of his gang members. He raked his fingers through his hair, his neck and cheeks burning hot, and turned back to face the screen. If it was Qiang, he was in danger. If he were to be found, the Imperial Police would surely shoot him on sight.

He quickly pulled out his Linq and furiously typed a message to Qiang: *Call me. Please.*

The camera zoomed in as the crowd around Director Shei's body slowly dispersed. Shiro's eyes landed on Ru—Shei's daughter—who held her mother's limp arm in her lap, blood soaking them both. Ru's eyes were red and full of rage as she screamed and sobbed. Avi's hands were on Ru's shoulders, trying to calm her down.

Shiro's attention was glued to the televiewer, his

anxiety at its peak as he waited for word of the attacker's capture. He constantly checked his Linq screen, but it didn't light up with any message. After several minutes, it was announced that no suspect could be found at this time, but the Imperial Police were calling in backup to investigate further.

As medics confirmed Director Shei's death, the cameras focused in on her daughter. Shiro swallowed hard as Ru flared her nostrils. Her tears mixed with her dark eye makeup, causing black streams to flow down her cheeks. Her straight, black hair framed her tense face as she turned toward one camera. Her jaw was clenched, and her chest heaved as her breaths came hard. And her glare was filled with the promise of vengeance.

Fifteen

Mayhara held her arms out from her sides and pushed out her crimson energy. For a moment, nothing happened. She gritted her teeth in frustration but kept pushing. She was the elite crimson mage. This was her calling, her purpose. She had to believe that she would have control of her powers when the time came to use them. There was no way it was destiny's plan that the comet that empowered Kashmeru's rise would also strip the good guys of their powers.

She adjusted her stance and took a few calming breaths. A breeze blew her hair back from her face. She could do this. She had to.

Running her fingers over her wristband and feeling the smooth surface of the garnet stone, she reached deep down inside herself and pulled up all the confidence she could muster. With the next breath she took, she held her hands out, palms facing the ground, and told herself it would work. The red glow in her hands felt warm. Repeating to herself that she could do it, she pushed out her powers, demanding the crimson elements that flowed from her palms to work with the earth.

The ground began to tremble, tiny pebbles bouncing along the surface of the soil. A feeling of gratification filled her, and she raised her hands. A cloud of dirt and debris rose from the ground like a fog and swirled around her. Faster and faster until her smile turned into laughter.

"That's impressive," came a voice.

All at once, the swirling cloud stopped and the dirt

dropped. Mayhara swung around to find Penny approaching.

"Sorry," Penny said, closing the distance between them. "I didn't mean to scare you. I see you've got your powers under control."

"Well, it's taking more effort than it's supposed to. Which makes me very uncomfortable."

"I get a feeling that's not the only thing that's been making you uncomfortable lately."

"What do you mean?"

Penny smirked. "I know we've all been focusing on the war against the Pishacha, but we'd have to be pretty oblivious not to have noticed the tension between you and Jae."

"Oh." Mayhara pursed her lips. "That."

Penny didn't push, and Mayhara relaxed a little.

"Yeah." Mayhara gave her a small shrug. "I don't know what's going on there."

"I thought the two of you were a hot item. I mean, I know he and Loni have history, but I see the way he looks at you."

Mayhara felt heat bloom in her cheeks. She also felt

strange that Penny—who was apparently a close friend of Loni's—sounded like she was rooting for Jae choosing her instead of Loni. "It doesn't matter. We're not really in a position to worry about relationships at the moment. We've kind of got bigger fish to fry."

Penny tilted her head. "Yeah. But, I mean, what are we doing all this for? When you think about it, we're fighting for all the things that make life worth living. Isn't *love* one of those things?"

Mayhara swallowed. *Love?* Was that what this thing was between her and Jae? She couldn't be sure. She only knew she'd never felt the way she felt about Jae with anyone else.

She looked up to find Penny studying her. For a moment, it looked like Penny was annoyed.

"Is everything all right?" Mayhara asked her.

Penny blinked and her frown disappeared. "Yeah. Sure." She cleared her throat. "Hey, tell me about your family. They're in the prison camps, right?"

Mayhara's brows pulled together from the quick subject change. "Um, yeah. My parents and my sisters."

"You must be really worried about them."

"I am." Mayhara crossed her arms over her chest. "But Darshana somehow got them moved under fake names so they couldn't be tied to me."

"Moved out of the prison camps?"

"No. Darshana couldn't manage that. She just arranged for them to be placed in a more low-key location. I don't even know which camp they're in."

Penny gave her a nod, but her gaze seemed far away.

"Why do you ask?"

Penny seemed to snap from her thoughts. "Oh, I'm just… I wanted to catch up with everyone and, you know, get to know you better. Understand your struggles."

"Oh. Okay. That's nice."

"Were your sisters at the academy too?" Penny suddenly asked.

Mayhara felt like her head was spinning, trying to keep up with Penny's train of thought. "Um, no. They were too young at the time. But my younger sister Kakoli would have started last year if the academy had still been open. I think she would have really enjoyed it. She's a bit of a showoff. I just hope she's not drawing attention to herself in the camps. For her own safety."

"If she's as level-headed as you, I'm sure she's lying low." Penny let out what sounded like a defeated sigh. "Well, I'll let you get back to training. Keep up the good work."

"Thanks." Mayhara watched as Penny turned and walked back toward the house, puzzled by her odd behavior. She wondered if something more had happened while Penny had been abducted. Something Penny wasn't ready to share with the rest of them.

⸙

Bhutano checked to make sure no one was around as he pulled out the Linq and pushed the button to contact Naree. The reflection in the window startled him for a second when he found Penny's eyes staring back at him. He pushed her hair away from her face and turned away from the window.

"Bhutano?"

"Hello."

"What's wrong?" Naree asked. "You sound troubled."

"I'm hitting a wall with the crimson elite. I can't seem

to crack into her mind to find the dagger."

"Do you think it's because of the comet's influence on the amethyst mage's powers?"

"No. I don't think so. Her defenses are strong. She's got some thick walls up. I just need more time."

"What about the others? The diamond or… sapphire?"

Bhutano's eyes narrowed when Naree had hesitated before referencing her brother. "I think I'll try the Sacred Key first. I have a feeling he'll be easier to wear down."

"All right. Um, Bhutano?"

"Yes, Your Highness?"

"When we were last on the property… There was a moment where we came near the house, and there was a point where we couldn't come any closer."

"What do you mean?"

"It was a protection spell, I think. You said they have a witch."

Though she couldn't see him, he nodded. "They do."

"She must have cast a spell to protect the house. We could only get so far before we hit a barrier."

"Strange." Bhutano rubbed at Penny's chin. "I guess I

was able to get through because I'm in the amethyst's body." Bhutano stood straighter. "Wait. Why were you coming close to the house?"

Naree was quiet for a moment. "No reason. Curiosity, perhaps."

"Don't do it again. We're getting far, but we can't afford to mess up this mission."

Again, silence filled the seconds. "Yes, I understand."

"I'll contact you when I find out where the next dagger is hidden. Until then, stick to the plan."

Sixteen

Mr. Kitaro handed the small scroll back to Karina. He scrubbed at his face as if trying to scrub away his frown. "I don't think we can risk melting the gold without damaging the scroll itself."

Karina bit the inside of her cheek. "So you think only magic will open it."

It wasn't a question, but Mr. Kitaro nodded anyway. "I'm sure that whatever witch spelled it shut meant for it to only be opened by another witch. Hence: Magic."

"I figured you'd say that." Karina sighed. "I guess I was just hoping for a Hail Mary or something. But deep down, I knew it was going to have to be magic."

A figure appeared in the doorway of Mr. Kitaro's room. "*What's* going to have to be magic?"

Mr. Kitaro tucked his hands behind his back. "Ah, Penny. How are you feeling?"

"I'm fine." Penny offered him a small smile. "Thanks for asking. What, uh, were you two talking about? If you don't mind me asking, that is."

"The small scroll," Mr. Kitaro answered.

"We still can't figure out how to open it," Karina added.

Penny's brow furrowed. "What scroll?"

Karina and Mr. Kitaro exchanged a look.

"My dear." Mr. Kitaro shook his head. "Did no one fill you in on the scroll Jae and Mayhara took from the grimoire?"

The color seemed to drain from Penny's face. Her jaw

dropped open as Karina held the scroll out for Penny to see.

"I can't believe we didn't tell you," Karina said. "You were still trapped by the Pishacha when Jae and Mayhara brought it back. With all the chaos and my grandmother's funeral, news about the scroll slipped through the cracks."

Penny's eyes were still on the scroll. "What do you mean *from* the grimoire?"

"It was hidden in the spine," Karina told her. "Mayhara managed to take it out before the dark mages stole the grimoire from the Bhaja Caves."

"What… What is it? What's it for?" Penny blinked rapidly as she pushed her hair out of her face.

Karina rolled the scroll in her hands. "Before my grandmother died, she said she got a message from our ancestors. The scroll apparently contains a spell that will destroy Kashmeru. Forever."

Penny flinched and swallowed hard. "What? I've never heard of such a thing. Are you… Are you sure?"

"Well, there's no way of telling for sure if anything's in here at all." Karina tapped the scroll against her palm. "Since we can't get it open."

"Okay." Penny nodded slowly, taking it all in. "So that's what you were talking about when you said it was going to take magic."

"Yes. But there's one more thing you probably should know." Karina pursed her lips and glanced at Mr. Kitaro.

"The spell," he said, "won't destroy only the dark god. Because the two deities are linked, it's believed the spell will destroy the Lotus as well."

Penny seemed to only be able to stare at Mr. Kitaro in disbelief. He took a step back and waited, giving her a minute to absorb the information.

"Right," Penny finally said. "Well, we don't want that."

"But if I could take a look at the spell," Karina said, "then I could make sure. Or maybe I could find a loophole."

Penny narrowed her eyes. "Good idea."

"But first, I'd need to open it." Karina turned toward the door. "Which I'm determined to figure out."

She gave them a curt wave before she left the room. Penny could only stare after her.

"We were pretty stunned when we found out as well."

Mr. Kitaro gave Penny an apologetic nod. "I'm sorry it took us so long to realize you weren't briefed on the whole situation. I thought for sure one of the others had already told you."

He placed a hand on her shoulder.

Penny turned to him. Though her smile seemed forced, her eyes seemed more in the present than they had been moments before. "I understand. I'm sure the others thought the same. So, um, did you not know about any of this? I mean, wasn't that something you learned as a Sacred Key?"

"No." Mr. Kitaro straightened his shirt. "There are still many mysteries associated with the legend. I had to learn a lot before I was handed the responsibility of protecting the dagger, but I have to be honest, a lot of what's come to light in the last couple of months is brand new information."

"I see."

"I'm surprised you didn't."

"Didn't what?"

"See." Mr. Kitaro gave her a wink. "Amethyst insight powers and all."

"Oh." She let out a small laugh. "It doesn't always work like that. And who knows? Maybe the comet's blocking my *vision*."

"Perhaps."

"And what about the concept of the new world Shiro talked about?"

"Are you asking if I heard of the theory when I became a Sacred Key?"

"Yes." Penny went to a nearby chair and sat down, crossing her legs. "What did you learn about it?"

"Throughout the centuries, there have been many theories of how Kashmeru's revenge would unfold. And yes, one of them was the idea that he would create a new realm in which to exist, a new world of his creation governed by his rules."

Penny studied his face. "Do you think it could be true?"

"I truly hope never to find out. Kashmeru needs to be stopped before destruction of *this* world ensues."

"But what if they're right?"

Mr. Kitaro's brows scrunched together. He shook his head. "If the worst happens, and Kashmeru triumphs, it's not a world I would want to be part of."

❧

Naree glanced at the screen of her Linq and stepped out onto the balcony to answer it. "Bhutano?"

"I have good news and bad news," came the reply.

It was a female voice, but Naree knew it was really Bhutano. It had taken her a while to get used to hearing him speaking with Penny's vocal cords.

"Let's have them, then," Naree said.

"I know where the next dagger is hidden."

Naree relaxed her shoulders a little. "Great."

"But the bad news is you won't be able to get to it. It's in the house. And because of the protection spell, it's off-limits to you."

"What's the plan, then?"

"There is an opportunity coming up when everyone should be out of the house. The meteor shower. The guru has a theory she wants to try out with the mages, something that has to do with the comet. Anyway, there's a hilltop on the property where we're all going to test this theory out the night of the meteor shower, and when we all head up there, I'll find an excuse to come back early and get the dagger then."

Naree nibbled on her pinky nail. "Are you sure you won't get caught? They could get suspicious if you slip away."

"I'll try to be convincing. They have no reason to suspect me of anything. I'm their very good friend Penny." Bhutano cleared his—or rather, Penny's—throat. "There's one more thing. When the grimoire was stolen, the elite mages took something that was hidden in the spine."

"Hidden?" Naree grabbed the strands of hair that were blowing in her face from the wind. "What was it?"

"It's a problem."

"Bhutano, come on."

"It's a small scroll. Miniature."

"I guess it would have to be to have been hidden in a book spine." She turned and headed back inside. "What's in the scroll?"

As he told her the scroll's purpose and how it could

mean her death, her skin became prickly and her stomach twisted in the tightest knot. Her mind felt as if it were being smothered in a thick, wet, itchy blanket.

"They won't use the spell," she insisted.

"How do you know?"

She hesitated. "Jae-hyun would never do anything to harm me, much less kill me."

"I think you might be underestimating your brother."

Naree raked her fingers through her hair, unable to fathom that Jae would simply sacrifice her to win the war. "So you plan to steal the scroll as well?"

"Yes. I've spoken to Kashmeru, and we agree that it's imperative. We don't want them having any advantage over us. We must do whatever it takes."

Seventeen

Shiro's breath left him for a long moment when Qian's name flashed on his Linq's screen. He couldn't push the button to accept the call fast enough.

"Qiang?"

"Shiro, I'm glad I caught you."

Shiro expelled a breath of relief. "Where are you? Are

you all right?" They weren't even half the questions Shiro wanted the answers for, but he could hardly hear past his heart thumping in his ears.

"I'm all right." Qiang was quiet for a moment. "As for where I am, I probably shouldn't say, just in case someone is listening."

Though Qiang couldn't see him, Shiro nodded. "All right. As long as you're okay. You can't imagine how tense I've been wondering if you've been captured by the Imperial Police."

"I take it you saw the funeral."

Shiro opened his mouth and then shut it again. He wanted so much to ask him if he was the one who'd killed Director Shei, but he wasn't sure if he could do it. It wasn't a defensive move or something done to save someone's life. It was a full-on attack. And Shiro didn't know if he could accept Qiang point-blank murdering someone. A part of him knew it wasn't the first murder Qiang could be involved in. There were bound to be fatalities in the bombings and vicious attacks the extremists had been responsible for. But there was something more personal in targeting Director Shei.

Something more direct in killing just one person in a moment of innocence.

"I did," Shiro said. "I saw it."

There was silence again, and somehow it was all Shiro needed to hear to know Qiang had done it.

"Any news on the camps?" Shiro asked instead.

"We were running into dead ends all over the place. Most of the mages who'd lost their powers couldn't tell us what had happened. But then we came upon a sapphire mage who'd used her powers to keep the truth untouched inside her head. She told us about two men coming to the camps. One of them would somehow drain the mages' powers, and the other would convince them to forget what had happened."

"She was able to resist them?"

"Yes. Somehow."

"She must be very skilled."

Shiro wondered if she might be close in line to be the next elite. The news also gave him hope that the elites might be able to fight off the powers of the one who was draining powers.

"And what about explosives?" Shiro asked.

"We found them at that camp and were able to disarm them. We would have never been able to find them if it hadn't been for that girl. We're going to check the other camps and see if they're using the same method of operation for hiding the explosives. I just don't know if we can find them all and disarm them before the government decides to use them."

Shiro raked a hand through his hair. "Okay. Be careful. Please."

It took a second before Qiang answered. "I will, Shiro. You too."

Darshana rubbed her temples. Something was off, but she couldn't be sure what it was. She knew she should meditate, but she felt as if the throbbing in her head wouldn't let her. It was almost as if someone were tapping on the back of her skull over and over, harder every minute, demanding her attention.

She went to the kitchen, hoping a peppermint tea

might help alleviate the ache. As the water kettle heated up, she heard footfalls approaching. She thought, at this late hour, everyone was already asleep—or at least in bed. So it surprised her to find Penny coming toward her.

"Is there enough hot water for two?" Penny asked.

"Plenty." Darshana took another mug out of the cabinet. "Why are you still up?"

"I was just thinking about the meteor shower. It's the day after tomorrow, right?"

"Yes."

Penny let out a small, humorless laugh. "I'm just so mixed up lately. Losing track of the days."

"It's understandable. We've been hiding out here for so long. And you were kidnapped. I can just imagine what that must have done to your head."

"Yeah." Penny looked through the cannisters and selected a tea. "I was thinking we should all stick together. You know, when we go up to the top of the hill for the meteor shower. Not just you and the mages, but all of us."

"Karina and Mr. Kitaro?"

"I think it would give us a real sense of being a team. One big, united front, supporting each other."

"Yes, that would be nice." Darshana filled their mugs with the boiling water. "Is that what was keeping you up?"

"Well, not just that." Penny stirred her tea. "I guess it's nerves. Wondering if my powers will hold out when it comes down to the, uh, big moment."

Darshana sighed. "Yes, I'm afraid your teammates are feeling the same apprehension. And that worries me. I need to find a way to boost your collective confidence. A big part of winning a battle is believing that you can."

Penny sipped her tea, studying Darshana's face. "Yes. I think you're right."

Don't, Darshana. It's a trap!

Penny tried with everything she could muster to get Bhutano to somehow slip up. To stutter. To drop the tea. Anything that might tip off Darshana that she was being duped. Time was running out. Darshana and the others were falling for every trick Bhutano was pulling. And the elites had everything to lose.

Eighteen

The sun had almost completely disappeared behind the horizon when the elite mages departed the house to begin their journey to the hilltop. Originally, only the elites and Darshana were going to go up to see the meteor shower, but Penny had insisted that they should all stick together, Karina and Mr. Kitaro included.

Karina had to admit, she was curious about how the meteors might affect the mages' powers. Plus, she'd only seen a meteor shower from the swamp, and the prospect of seeing one from the top of a high hill made her a bit excited.

The excitement was what kept her moving. The first half of the walk had been manageable, but once they started climbing the slope of the hill, Karina's legs began to feel the burn. She distracted herself from the ache by listening to Penny asking Jae about what it had been like growing up with the Lotus as a sister. Their conversation took up a good portion of the ascent, and Karina felt she learned a lot about Jae she hadn't known before.

By the time they'd reached their destination, the night sky was littered with millions of stars. The Akutake comet was visible, making its prophesized approach. Darshana had laid out a large picnic blanket and sat cross-legged as she watched the sky. Karina sat beside her, leaning back on her hands. Mr. Kitaro had a small notepad in his hand and a pen in the other, ready to jot down any changes that might occur in the mages' magic.

Shiro seemed to be scoping the sky for clouds, prepared to lend a hand of moving any nebulous obstacle out of the way, if his powers would allow him to. Salina pointed out something—a constellation, Karina thought she'd heard—to Mayhara. The speculation was that the three of them might be more directly affected by the comet and the meteors than the others would. The meteors were comprised of dust and rock fallout from previous comets, the comet itself was ice at its core, and they all were inflicted with fire burning away at them as they made their journey through space.

Of course, Loni had argued that they all traveled through air, meaning they were deeply connected to her as well. But Yuki had debunked her theory by reminding everyone that there was no air in space. It was a vacuum. She went further to say that sound waves could not travel through a vacuum; therefore, Jae's connection was also not as strong as the crimson, copper, and golden elites'.

"It's starting," Salina said. She stared, wide-eyed, as a pair of meteors shot across the sky. She stuck her hands in the back pockets of her jeans and smiled. "Whoa!"

"The idea was not to enjoy a show," Darshana called

out. "It was to test out your powers during the shower to see if they improve."

"But how will that help us?" Loni asked. "I mean, when we're trying to fight off the Pishacha and keep Kashmeru in his tomb."

"Perhaps our crimson mage could replicate such a celestial event," Darshana said, "to give us an edge."

Everyone turned to Mayhara, whose expression suggested this was the first she'd heard of the idea.

Salina pulled her hands out of her pockets and blew out a breath. "Right. Let's do this."

Taking it upon herself to go first, Salina planted her feet in a defensive stance. She pushed out her palms in front of her, her fingers visibly taut.

Karina watched as Salina focused on her hands, seemingly pushing out her energy. It seemed like the seconds were ticking by with nothing happening. And then finally, a spark appeared, and two seconds later, a fireball shot from her hands and zoomed across the hilltop, barely missing a tree.

Karina wasn't sure if this was better or worse than what Salina had been experiencing since the comet had started interfering with her powers, but Mr. Kitaro must have had an idea, as he scribbled furiously onto his notepad.

As Shiro took his turn, Penny slid over quietly to Darshana and put a hand on her knee.

"Will you forgive me if I head back to the house?" Penny grimaced as she waited for Darshana's answer.

"Is everything all right?"

"I've been hit with a terrible migraine. And I know it was me who suggested we make a team effort out of tonight, but I think I need to lie down."

Darshana studied her face. "Do you think it's because of the meteor shower?"

"It could be." Penny glanced at the sky. "I was fine until I came up here."

Darshana offered her a small smile. "Of course, dear. Will you be all right going alone? Or should I send someone with you?"

"No, I'll be fine." Penny patted her knee. "I just need darkness and silence and my pillow."

"All right." Darshana nodded. "We'll see you later. Feel better, dear."

"Thank you. And good luck with your tests."

Karina gave Penny a nod and watched as she left. She wondered if it was the combination of the comet and the meteors affecting Penny's head, attacking the base of her powers where her visions and insight manifested.

A bright white light flashed out of the corner of her eye and drew her focus away from Penny's descent down the hill. She turned to see a sparkling dome of diamonds shielding Yuki. Yuki had a look of intense concentration on her face.

"Seems to be working," Karina said to Darshana.

Darshana pursed her lips. "It's taking more effort. More time. I thought perhaps the layer of debris between the mages and the comet might throw off the disruption, but I can see now the comet is too strong."

"What does that mean?"

"It's not good." Darshana blinked slowly. "But I'm going to have to trust that my mages can pull through when it counts."

Karina breathed in deeply, exhaling as she watched Mayhara forming crimson bullets and shooting them off the hilltop. The sound of each bullet rung in her ears. The ringing intensified, and Karina flinched as the sounds merged into one high-pitched tone.

As the ringing wavered, Karina swore she heard a whisper. She narrowed her eyes, trying to concentrate on the voice.

"…the scroll!"

She placed her hands over her ears, confused by the voice. She grit her teeth and listened harder.

"Don't… the scroll!"

Karina's eyes shot to Darshana, who was watching her with a curious gaze. A strange pull stung in Karina's chest. She sprang to her feet.

"What is it?" Darshana's eyes flit over her face.

"I don't know." Her breaths came quickly. "Something about the scroll."

"About how to open it?"

Karina shook her head. "I'm not sure. But something's… It doesn't feel right. Something's telling me to go to it. I need to keep it near me. To keep it secure."

Darshana sat up straighter, uncrossing her legs. "Are you hearing a voice?"

Karina nodded as she released a shuddered breath.

Darshana gestured with her head. "Then you must listen. Go on. We'll catch up later."

With a wildly thumping heart, Karina turned and hurried back to the house.

Nineteen

Bhutano's breaths came hard as he approached the house. Tonight, he would kill three birds with one stone. He cut off the Linq call to Naree, having successfully delivered the message as to where the sapphire elite had hidden his dagger. Jae's mind had opened up to Penny so easily when asked about growing up with his sister. It was almost too easy to search his mind and find the dagger's hiding place. He thanked the fates that Jae's dagger wasn't in the house. Naree and the dark mages would only have to travel to a small musical instrument shop on the outskirts of New Jaipur, where Jae had concealed the dagger inside the casing of an amplifier. Bhutano was positive Naree would have no trouble finding it. Though he still hadn't pinned down the location of Mayhara's dagger, he did manage to see the location of the dagger the Sacred Key had hidden. He'd just have to retry his manipulation technique with the crimson elite mage later. For now it was up to him to get Mr. Kitaro's dagger and find the scroll.

The house was dark. Bhutano checked behind him to make sure no one was coming. He tried to use Penny's power of insight to his advantage, but he wasn't getting any visions. He wondered if the comet might be affecting the amethyst mage's powers after all.

He didn't have any time to waste. With a sense of urgency, he headed straight for Mr. Kitaro's office and switched on the small desk lamp. There was a screwdriver waiting for him in the desk drawer. Bhutano had placed it there earlier so it would be accessible, especially considering the time constraint.

Screwdriver in hand, he dropped to his knees and pried the tool between the two floorboards he'd seen in Mr. Kitaro's mind. The boards loosened easier than he'd guessed, and in a matter of seconds, a black box with a shiny red and gold design was staring back at him. He gently pulled the box from its hiding place. He could hear Kashmeru singing his praises in his head. It wouldn't be practical to take the whole box, so Bhutano opened it and removed the dagger. The blade glinted, even in the low light of the desk lamp.

After tucking the dagger into the inside pocket of Penny's jacket, Bhutano returned the box and moved the floorboards back into place.

Step one was complete. Next step: the scroll.

Bhutano switched off the desk lamp and quietly exited the office. He paused in the hall and listened but was met by nothing but silence. The mages were surely busy testing their powers at the top of the hill, and he believed they'd be there for another hour, at least. Still, he should hurry and get the job done.

Continuing on to Karina's room, he clicked on the light and scanned the area. "Where are you keeping it, little witch?" he whispered.

Careful not to make a mess of anything, he rifled through drawers and checked the bookshelf. A buzzing suddenly went off in his head, and he froze.

Someone was coming.

Bhutano quickly flipped off the light and backed up, squeezing into a space between a cabinet and a corner of the room. Anyone coming into the room wouldn't be able to see that someone was there.

He held his breath as the door opened and Karina walked in. She didn't seem to be aware of anything except for the reason she'd come into the room.

She grabbed a wicker bag that hung on the back of a chair. Reaching into the bag, she pulled out the scroll. Bhutano grit his—or rather, Penny's—teeth, furious that he hadn't checked the bag.

Kill her.

The sound of Kashmeru's voice made Bhutano flinch.

Kill her and take the scroll. She could destroy me with that spell. She could ruin everything.

Bhutano swallowed, realizing Kashmeru was right. He had the opportunity to stop her right there in that moment. No one else was around. He could convince the others, as Penny, that someone had broken in and attacked her. Pishacha or a dark mage, for example. He could claim they'd stolen the scroll. He could even fake an injury as proof that Penny had tried to stop them. They wouldn't have any reason to doubt Penny.

Bhutano reached inside the jacket's inside pocket and pulled out the dagger. He took a quiet step forward as Karina stuffed the scroll into a small canvas satchel. She hung the satchel over her shoulder, the strap crossing diagonally over her chest.

Bhutano raised the dagger, high over his head, ready to pounce.

The door suddenly swung open again, and Bhutano almost gasped. He promptly reverted back into the corner, pressing against the wall to keep out of sight.

Karina turned toward the door. "Shiro?"

"I was worried when I saw you leave the hilltop," he said. "Darshana told me you needed to get the scroll, so I thought I'd make sure you were okay."

She patted the satchel. "Yeah, I got it. I can't explain it; it's like I feel like it's precious cargo. I think I need to keep it on me."

"Probably a good idea."

"But you didn't have to leave the hilltop. I'm all right."

"I did, though." He offered her a small smile. "I promised Amalia I'd take care of you. I owe her that much."

"Thank you." She returned his smile. "We can head back up if you want. Is the meteor shower over yet?"

"I think Jae said we've got about another half hour or so."

"Great. Let's go." She ran her fingers down the strap as if making sure it was secure.

As they switched off the light and closed the door behind them, Bhutano let out a breath and stepped out from his hiding spot.

Get the scroll. It's imperative.

Bhutano cursed under his breath. He'd missed his opportunity and let down his god. But now he knew where the scroll would be at all times. He'd get another chance. And he wouldn't screw it up next time.

Twenty

Yuki sat in the meadow, closing her eyes as the sun broke through the clouds. The grass touched her legs, making them a little itchy, but she tried to ignore the sensation and concentrate. They would be leaving in a few days to infiltrate the Lotus temple and usurp the enemy's plans. And she wasn't sure if she was ready. Darshana wanted them to be in the right mindset for their upcoming battle, so Yuki decided to meditate. The flowers in the meadow caused a pleasant fragrance to waft through the air. It helped to calm her mind.

Breathing deeply, she reached down into the source of her power. Theoretically, a mage whose power included controlling emotions should be able to keep everyone confident, including herself. Maybe it was the comet's interference, but she was having a hard time managing the elites' moods. And what made it worse was that she could feel her own confidence plummeting along with everyone else's. But she had to believe she could overcome it.

She had to.

Something in the air changed. A different emotion, like waves of something darker entering her vibration.

She opened her eyes.

"Don't mind me," Penny said. "I was just taking a walk to clear my mind."

"That's okay." Yuki smiled and patted the ground beside her. "That's why I'm here too."

Penny returned her smile as she crouched down and sat beside her. Yuki told herself the dark emotion she felt from Penny must have been her doubt, which was understandable. A part of her feared Penny might have seen something with her amethyst powers—something about the outcome of their situation—and she wasn't telling them. It would explain why Penny's dark emotions were much grimmer than the others'.

"I take it you're worried about this showdown too," Penny said.

Yuki twisted her lips. "I hate to admit it, but yeah."

"I was hoping you might have a better influence on our spirits. We could really use it."

"Believe me, I'm trying." Yuki shifted, tucking her legs underneath herself. "It's like there's this looming cloud, filled with heaviness and uncertainty, pressing down on us, and I'm fighting to clear it. Because I know if I do, we can come out on top."

Penny nodded. "And things have been complicated for you too."

"What do you mean?"

"I saw your expression when Avi appeared on screen during Min's funeral. And when Shei was hit, you jumped in your skin. Something made me think maybe part of you was worried Avi might have been hurt too."

Yuki furrowed her brow. She wasn't sure how she had felt about that. "No. I think I was just shocked by the unexpected attack."

"And if it had been *Avi* who'd been attacked?"

Yuki blinked in puzzlement. "I don't know. I mean, when I found out he was a follower of Kashmeru, it pretty much cut off all romantic feelings I had for him." She bit the inside of her cheek. "I mean, most of those feelings, anyway."

Penny tilted her head. "You never told me how you met."

"Didn't I?"

Yuki carried the tray of coffee, zigzagging through the people crowding the city streets. She'd been working for a kimono designer who thankfully didn't ask a lot of questions about her past. Being so young, she didn't have much as far as office skills, but the designer and her staff were adamant coffee drinkers, so Yuki found herself making coffee runs at least three times a day. She didn't mind. They paid her enough credits to rent a tiny, one-

room apartment, and they often had enough leftover takeout that she didn't have to worry about feeding herself.

It had been almost two years since the Eradication. Two years since the government had abolished the academy and taken her into custody, proposing she work for them in order to keep her family safe. But her powers had told her they were lying, and so she'd fled when the opportunity had arisen. The next thing she knew, her parents had been killed.

Of course, something told her that they would have been killed anyway, at some point.

On the run and fearing for her life, she used her powers to land herself a meaningless job, changed the cut and color of her hair, and kept herself out of sight from the Imperial Police as much as she could.

So when she saw a police officer in her path on her way back to the kimono studio from the coffee shop, she quickly turned on her heel to change direction.

And smacked right into a young man, nearly dropping all the coffee.

"I'm so sorry," she blubbered, readjusting her grip on the carrier tray. If she had lost even one coffee, she'd have to go back to replace it or have to face the wrath of one of her bosses.

"No, it's my fault," the young man said. He had a boyish face and spikey hair that Yuki found interesting.

"How is it your fault?" She laughed. "I practically clobbered you with six liters of caffeine."

"Yeah, that seems like a lot for such a petite young lady."

"It's not all for—" She let out another laugh, caught off guard by his amazing eyes.

"I know." He flashed a smile that made her blush. "So who are you running away from?"

Her eyes widened. "What? No, I'm not… uh… What makes you say that?"

"I'm pretty good at reading body language."

Normally, she would have rolled her eyes at the line, but her emotion sensors weren't setting off any red flags. He was genuinely interested in her. "Okay, you got me. I'm… avoiding someone. But I've got to get this to my *bosses, so I'm taking a detour."*

He studied her face and bit his lip. "Well, how would you feel about company?"

"What?" She almost giggled.

"It's the least I could do for almost making you spill all that coffee. I'll escort you safely to your destination, coffee intact, and in return I get to enjoy the pleasure of refreshing conversation."

"And he walked with you the whole way back?" Penny asked.

"He did." She sighed. "And he wasn't creepy or anything. He was actually charming and kind of funny. Which is why I went out with him a few times after that. But then, on one date, we overheard these university kids discussing deities. And when Kashmeru's name came up, Avi started acting strange. He made some off comments and mumbled about how they were idiots who didn't understand the world. I got a real bad vibe when I read his emotions. That's when I figured out whose side he was really on."

Penny shifted as if she were uncomfortable. "That's

when you ended things?"

"I had to. Plus, I found out he was the governor's son. You can just imagine how complicated that could get. But bigger than that, how could I keep seeing someone with such screwed-up ideologies?"

Yuki's thoughts flashed in her head: finding out the truth about Avi, the dark mages, her need to be strong in the battle, and keeping the daggers out of the reach of the enemy.

Penny's eyes narrowed for a second. Yuki felt a chill run up and down her spine. Something wasn't right.

"You're right," Penny said. She stretched and got to her feet. "No one should have to compromise their beliefs." She glanced over her shoulder. "I'm going to head back to the house. I'll see you later."

With a wave, Penny departed. Yuki felt as if her stomach were being eaten away by acid. Penny's emotions didn't match her expression. Yuki couldn't figure out what was happening, but she knew it wasn't good.

Twenty-One

Mayhara paced Karina's room while Karina attempted to make a list of every spell she knew. It was just a few days before they'd be leaving for New Delhi, and Mayhara felt dreadfully unprepared.

"Why can't I get this skepticism out of my head?" Mayhara asked, not really expecting Karina to answer.

"We have all the daggers, and even if Jae's theory is correct, there's no guarantee the Pishacha's witch can even unlock Kashmeru's tomb. And even if she does, we have a spell that could destroy him for good."

"Except that I can't get the scroll with the spell open," Karina rebutted.

The door to Karina's room opened, and Mayhara turned to see Yuki walk in. There was a strange look on her face, and she was wringing her hands.

"Yuki?" Mayhara stopped pacing. "What's wrong?"

Yuki looked over her shoulder. "Not here," she whispered. "Would you two like to go for a walk with me?"

The look in Yuki's eyes told Mayhara that whatever was on her mind couldn't wait. Mayhara and Karina exchanged a look, and Karina nodded. In silence, they gathered their things. Karina already had the satchel with the scroll slung around her. None of them said a word as they made their way through the house and out the front door. Mayhara was grateful they hadn't run into anyone along the way.

Mayhara couldn't help but wonder whom Yuki was

trying to prevent from hearing their conversation. She almost suggested that they get Jae so he could use his powers to soundproof them as they spoke, but then she wondered if it might be Jae's ears Yuki was trying to get away from. She hoped it wasn't.

They walked for what seemed like miles, with Yuki constantly looking over her shoulder. They were on a path that went through a thick forest of khair and sandalwood trees, hidden from view so no one would spot them. Mayhara could hear the babble of a nearby stream. The air was colder here, and Mayhara shivered.

"There's something… wrong." Yuki stopped and turned to them. Her arms were wrapped around herself.

"What is it?" Karina asked.

Yuki tucked her hair away from her face. "It's Penny."

Mayhara flashed her a questioning look. "What about her?"

Yuki shook her head. "I can't be sure. We were talking, and something strange happened. She was being friendly, but everything I felt coming from her was anger, rage, and vengeance."

At first Mayhara simply gaped at her, but then she

recalled something that had happened. "She and I had a conversation recently too, and she was acting really strange. She kept asking me questions."

"What kind of questions?" Yuki asked.

"About me and Jae. About my family and which prison camp they were in. I couldn't make heads or tails of why she was being so inquisitive. And she kept switching topics, like she was trying to get me to say something in particular."

Karina's eyes widened. "*Don't. The scroll.*"

"What?" Yuki and Mayhara asked her at the same time. Karina let out a shuddered breath, her hand tightening on the strap of her satchel. "I've been hearing a voice lately. In my head. At first I thought it was my brain's way of grieving, but now I think it's actually my grandmother speaking to me from… wherever she is."

"Speaking to you about what?" Mayhara asked.

"I could only get a few words. The first few times it was 'deceiving you.' And then, then other night, on the hilltop, it was 'Don't. The scroll.' The sentences were broken up, so I had to piece things together myself." Karina patted the satchel. "That's why I left that night to get the scroll. I've been keeping it at my side ever since."

"But why would Penny be lying to us?" Mayhara's forehead was scrunched up so much, it began to ache. "Why would she want the scroll?"

"Thinking back," Yuki said as she paced back and forth in a short line next to them, "things started to get weird ever since she showed up here after being captured by the Pishacha."

"Yeah." Mayhara tapped her chin. "That in and of itself was strange. I think we were so grateful that she'd returned we simply accepted that she'd easily escaped and found us with no trouble. With no one chasing her."

"So, what are we saying?" Karina worried the satchel strap, her eyes darting between the other two young women.

"That Penny switched sides?" Mayhara asked.

"Or..." Yuki visibly swallowed. "That Penny isn't... Penny."

"What?" Karina scoffed. "What does that even mean?"

"The police chief. Min." Mayhara practically slapped a hand against her mouth as the pieces started to come together. "He was being possessed by Bhutano—

Kashmeru's spirit messenger. Loni and Salina said that right before Min died, he grabbed Penny. That black smoke escaped his body just before he fell to the floor."

"You think Bhutano's spirit left Min and transferred to Penny?" Karina asked.

"It fits," Yuki said. "It explains all the strange ways she was acting."

"So it's not Penny," Mayhara said. "It's Bhutano. This whole time. But what was he doing? Biding his time? Why didn't he just kill us all when he had the chance?"

"Because he needed something from us." Yuki's eyes widened. "The daggers."

"But Penny—I mean, Bhutano," Mayhara corrected herself, "never asked me anything about the scrolls."

"An amethyst mage wouldn't have to." Karina narrowed her eyes in thought. "She'd just have to get you talking so the defenses of your mind were lowered enough that she could slip in there and find out the information for herself."

"I don't know what scares me more," Mayhara said. "That Bhutano is able to use Penny's powers or that our daggers could all be gone."

The three of them gawked at each other as the revelation sunk in.

"But what about Penny?" Yuki asked. "The real Penny, I mean."

"She's probably still in there," Karina said. "Judging from what I know about possessions."

"So how do we get her out?" Yuki shook her head. "How do we rescue her?"

"You don't," said a figure, stepping onto the path.

Twenty-Two

Karina and the others quickly huddled together, raising their hands to defend themselves. Karina's fist clenched around the satchel strap as she struggled to keep her knees from buckling.

Penny—whom they now knew to be Bhutano—smirked at them. In that moment, Karina could no longer see the person before her as Penny. Though it looked like her, it was the enemy, Kashmeru's henchman, they were dealing with now.

Bhutano was not alone, she came to realize. Waltzing up to stand behind him were Avi—the dark mage—and a Pishacha soldier dressed in black.

"Well, well, well," Avi said with a smirk. "Look what we've got here."

"I have to admit," Bhutano began, "that I didn't expect you lot to figure out my secret. But I guess we're all full of surprises, aren't we?"

"This isn't over," Mayhara said.

Bhutano raised a brow. "Is that what you believe? It looks like Kashmeru's side is at an advantage now. I don't see what hand you think you have to play."

"You won't win," Yuki said. "Evil never does."

Bhutano let out a laugh. "You are a delusional child. Do you know that? Just admit that we're better at this than you are."

"By tricking us all into revealing where all the daggers were hidden?" Mayhara scoffed. "That's why you kept hounding me with all those questions. To find out where

I'd kept my dagger."

Bhutano smiled through Penny's face. "Actually, it didn't work on you. Until now, that is. Thank you, crimson mage, for letting me into your mind. Now I have everything I want." He pointed at Karina. "Except for that."

Karina gasped and backed up, her hands covering the satchel Bhutano pointed at.

"In fact, we'll take you as well, little witch." Bhutano looked her up and down. "You've absorbed your grandmother's powers. I can just imagine the magic you now possess. Releasing Kashmeru's tomb should be a walk in the park for you."

Karina bared her teeth. "You'll have to kill me first."

Bhutano smirked. "Ask and it shall be granted. Avi?"

Avi glared at Karina and stepped forward. He raised his hand and lowered his chin. A burst of black cloud formed in his palm. They'd called this dark mage the bone crusher, and Karina's heart felt as if it were about to leap out of her chest in fear.

"No, Avi! Don't!" Yuki screamed. She stepped in front of Karina and raised both hands. Gritting her teeth, she released a barrage of diamond bullets. Mayhara and Karina ducked down, covering their heads.

Avi jerked back, gripping his shoulder. Blood pooled at his side as well. The sneer didn't leave his face as he stumbled back and fell to the ground.

It had happened so fast, Karina had missed it, but the Pishacha soldier was gone. Only a small puff of black smoke could be seen where he had been, so Karina couldn't be sure whether he had been struck or not.

Bhutano had been knocked back into a tree. He pressed against a gushing wound on his upper arm and squared his jaw. "You'd really sacrifice your friend? Avi never mentioned how brutal you were, little girl."

The look on Yuki's face told Karina she hadn't meant to hit Penny's body with the bullet. Yuki trembled, shaking her head as she backed up. Karina wanted to go to Penny and stop the bleeding. If Penny was still in there, she didn't want her to be hurt. She knew a spell. She would just have to put her hands on her and recite it.

"Let me help." Karina's voice sounded desperate as she raised her hands. "I can close the wound."

Bhutano narrowed his eyes, panting in pain, back

pressed against the tree as Karina approached. Karina kept her eyes on Bhutano's, hoping he would let her get close enough to help Penny.

Just as she reached him, she felt a hard jerk on her shoulder. With a gasp, she swung around to find Avi, who had crawled toward her and snatched the satchel from her shoulder, ripping the strap. Before she could stop herself, Karina flung herself at Avi, her hands closing in around the satchel. They both fell to the ground. Avi screamed in pain as Karina landed on his wounds.

Karina stumbled to her knees and flung the bag toward Yuki and Mayhara. As Mayhara caught the bag, Avi sprung to his feet and ran at her. Yuki's hands began to glow white.

Karina pointed her palms at Yuki and Mayhara, a spell spilling from her lips. The next moment seemed to go by in slow motion. A wave of energy pulsated outward from Karina's hands. Yuki and Mayhara were engulfed in a white light that emanated from Yuki's palms. Avi jumped and dived at Mayhara, his hands aiming for the satchel. As Karina shouted the last words of her spell, Yuki's white light intensified. Karina had to shield her eyes from the flash.

Suddenly, everything was much quieter. Karina opened her eyes. The spot where Mayhara and Yuki had been standing was empty. They were gone. With the scroll.

But so was Avi.

Karina's breaths were hard and heavy. She scanned the area, wondering what might have happened. Her spell was supposed to move them to safety, but she could only surmise that whatever magic Yuki had been generating had melded with her spell and cast them off somewhere else. But she didn't know where. And they were not alone.

She quickly turned to check if Bhutano was still there. She found him still backed up against the tree but slunk down a bit.

"What have you done?" he asked, cringing from his wound. "Where are they?"

Karina pressed her lips together, refusing to answer. Not that she could.

She jumped when a pop of smoke erupted beside Bhutano. The Pishacha soldier was back. The soldier bent to help Bhutano stand. Karina felt as if she were frozen as she watched the two of them. If she could just snap out of her shock and get her legs to move, she'd be able to run back to the house and warn the others.

"Let's get back to the Lotus," Bhutano said to the soldier. "We'll figure things out from there." He eyed Karina. "And bring the witch."

The story continues in

Diamond Mage

TURN THE PAGE
FOR A
PREVIEW OF
DIAMOND MAGE,
BOOK SEVEN
IN THE
EMPIRE OF THE LOTUS
SERIES

One

Darshana tensed her muscles, a rush of adrenaline coursing through her as her pulse hammered in her throat. She grit her teeth, pacing the main room of the house, as her heightened senses set off alarms in her head.

Danger.

Her mind raced, trying to make sense of the overload

of images ripping through her head. Her breaths came hard and fast as she tried to see and hear everything at once, but the visions were muddled, unclear, and she found it hard to put them in the right order.

"Darshana?"

She flinched, as if the voice knocked her from her thoughts. Wringing her hands, she gave an apologetic bow to Mr. Kitaro. "I'm sorry."

"What's wrong?" he asked, studying her. "Has something happened?"

"I believe so." She solemnly shook her head. "But I can't make heads nor tails of it."

Mr. Kitaro glanced over his shoulder, seemingly unsure of what to do.

"Check on the elites." The words barely left Darshana's lips before she darted toward the bedrooms.

Mr. Kitaro followed, and they each knocked on and opened the doors down the long hallway, calling out the names of the others.

Loni wrinkled her brow as she came to the door and met the anxiousness in Darshana's eyes.

"What's wrong?" Salina's eyes were wide with concern

as she stepped out into the hall.

Jae and Shiro soon joined her, obvious confusion on their faces.

"Did something happen?" Jae asked. "Is it Naree?"

Darshana slowly turned to them, her gaze intense as she pressed her fingertips together. "Where are the others? Mayhara, Yuki, Penny, and Karina?"

The others exchanged glances.

"They're not in the house? But it's dark outside." Salina marched toward the kitchen.

Loni furrowed her brow and darted toward the front door, leaving it open as she ran outside.

Jae whipped out his Linq. Shiro did the same. Darshana pressed her fingertips to her lips and forced herself to keep her breathing steady.

"Mayhara's Linq goes straight to voicemail," Jae said after pressing his Linq to his ear for a moment.

"Yuki's as well," Shiro added.

Salina returned from the main room, chewing on a nail. "Are they out training? Not that we're panicking for no reason?"

"This late at night?" Shiro asked.

"Maybe they wanted to test their powers again." Salina shook her head, as if she knew her theory was unlikely.

Loni stomped back into the house. "I can't see them anywhere."

Darshana's hands were clammy, the hairs lifting from the nape of her neck. "No. They're in trouble. I can feel it."

"But where are they?" Mr. Kitaro asked. "The property is big, but they can't have gotten far."

"Maybe you're forgetting," Loni said to him, "that the Pishacha can travel in clouds of smoke. They could have easily popped in for an attack and left again."

"We'll need to search the property, then," Mr. Kitaro rubbed a hand across his jaw. "If they're injured and lying out in one of the fields—"

"No." Darshana held her palms against her cheeks, her eyes narrowing. "No, they're not on the property. They're far. And I can't be sure, but I feel as if their energy is dispersed."

"Dispersed?" Jae asked.

"Like they're not together?" Shiro asked.

"You think they were kidnapped?" Salina asked.

Loni squared her jaw. "It wouldn't be the first time."

"What do we do?" Salina asked.

"Well, whatever we decide—" Mr. Kitaro's glance darted between them all. "—we can't stay here."

Salina blinked rapidly. "What?"

Darshana let out a sigh, her brows drawn together. "We have to come to terms with the fact that we've most likely been compromised. If the Pishacha have indeed kidnapped the others—or worse—then we cannot remain here as sitting targets for another attack."

Mr. Kitaro suddenly flinched, as if something troubling occurred to him. He turned on his heel and bolted into his office. Darshana exchanged looks with Jae. In a matter of seconds, Mr. Kitaro reappeared in the hall.

"It's gone," he said, color draining from his face.

"What is?" Salina asked.

"The dagger I was in charge of." He swallowed hard. "It's been stolen."

Darshana worried the knuckles of one hand. "I have a feeling it's not the only one missing."

Loni pressed her fingertips to her temples and let out a curse.

"We can check." Salina's hands clenched into fists. "Take inventory to see where we stand. But then what? What do we do? Where do we go?"

Darshana inhaled deeply, pushing down her panic. "We need to try to locate the others. To figure out how to rescue them. I can feel they need us. But in the meantime, we'll move on towards the Lotus temple. It's earlier than originally planned, I know. But it's the next logical step."

"And then what?" Shiro asked.

"And then we hope the gods have blessed us with a miracle to win this war."

READ MORE OF DIAMOND MAGE

The final book in the

Empire of the Lotus

series

AVAILABLE March 30, 2021

From Snowy Wings Publishing

In case you missed them…

Be sure to check out first five books in the

Empire of the Lotus series:

Available from all online retailers

CRIMSON MAGE

http://books2read.com/crimsonmage

COPPER MAGE

http://books2read.com/coppermage

GOLDEN MAGE

http://books2read.com/goldenmage

EMERALD MAGE

http://books2read.com/emeraldmage

SAPPHIRE MAGE

http://books2read.com/sapphiremage

ACKNOWLEDGEMENTS

The journey that I've been on while writing this book has been filled with many emotions. This past year has changed the world, and I think we're all still trying to find our footing.

In turbulent times, I have to pause and be thankful to all those who support not only me but others as well. Those who lift others up and try to unite us all as one.

Thank you to my family, friends, colleagues, my agent, my fellow authors, and of course my loyal readers. I do this all for you.

ABOUT THE AUTHOR

Dorothy Dreyer is a Philippine-born American living in Germany with her husband, her two college kids, and two Siberian Huskies. She is an award-winning, *USA Today* Bestselling Author of young adult and new adult books that usually have some element of magic or the supernatural in them. Aside from reading, she enjoys movies, binge-watching series, chocolate, take-out, traveling, and having fun with friends and family.

You can find out more about Dorothy on her website: http://dorothydreyer.com

Like YA Fantasy?

Check out the award-winning CURSE OF THE

PHOENIX duology:

PHOENIX DESCENDING

http://books2read.com/phoenixdescending

**Solo Medalist winner of the 2018 New Apple
Summer eBook awards in the category
Young Adult Fantasy**

Who must she become in order to survive?

Since the outbreak of the phoenix fever in Drothidia, Tori Kagari has already lost one family member to the fatal disease. Now, with the fever threatening to wipe out her entire family, she must go against everything she believes in order to save them—even if that means making a deal with the enemy.

When Tori agrees to join forces with the unscrupulous Khadulians, she must take on a false identity in order to infiltrate the queendom of Avarell and fulfill her part of the bargain, all while under the watchful eye of the unforgiving Queen's Guard. But time is running out, and every lie, theft, and abduction she is forced to carry out may not be enough to free her family or herself from death.

And ...

Also from Snowy Wings Publishing

When Darkness Whispers

by Heather L. Reid

https://www.snowywingspublishing.com/book/when-darkness-whispers/

It's time to choose: Love or lies, faith or fear, darkness or destiny.

Quinn Taylor hasn't slept through the night in months. Not since the demons from her dreams began materializing in the school hallway, feeding on her fears, and whispering of her death. Trading in her cheerleading uniform for caffeine drinks to keep the nightmares at bay, Quinn's life is in ruins from the demons' torment until Aaron, an amnesiac with a psychic ability, accidentally enters her dreams. He's the light in her darkness and she's the key to his past, but the last thing the demons want is for them to be together.

To keep them apart, the demons must convince Quinn that Aaron will betray her or, worse, confirm her fear that she's crazy. Aaron and Quinn's combined powers could banish the darkness for good, but only if she learns to trust her heart and he recovers the secret locked away in his fragile memory. That is, unless the demons kill them first.

finds an escape from the reality of planning her life after high school. But will it come at the cost of alienating Cora's mother, who struggles with her own tragic memories?

As the summer wanes, it becomes apparent that Mrs. O'Leary is desperate to leave Oyster Beach. And Ronan just may hold the answer to her tragic past— and Cora's future.

death.

Swept off her feet and growing in power, Ember will do anything for her undead boyfriend. But Ivy vows to put a stop to the paranormal mayhem before their newly blended family loses a daughter.

Will the two young women forge peace between warring magical worlds… or die for the ones they love?

Aqua

by Tracy Korn

https://books2read.com/u/b62XVM

Hold your breath…

The future is three miles underwater, and Jazwyn Ripley's time has come.

Earth's atmosphere will only support a few more generations, and most of advanced society has already relocated to the sea. To survive, only one option remains for the Topsiders—get into Gaia Sur, the elite academy on the ocean floor.

But after Jazwyn Ripley trains a lifetime for the chance, something is wrong in the interviews. Her evaluation isn't like those of her soul-rattled classmates, and now, Arco Hart is desperate to protect her from something he won't talk about.

Cryptic messages coming from the earth's core. A charming, but infamous rival who knows why.

Everything is telling her to walk away, but for the struggling class at the bottom, there's nowhere to go but down.

The road to everything the cadets ever wanted turns out to lead somewhere they never intended to go, and one decision will change the course of their lives for good:

Continue on the scripted path, or chase something deeper?

KILL ME ONCE, KILL ME TWICE

by Clara Kensie

https://books2read.com/KMOKMT

Lily Summerhays remembers how she died in each of her past lives. Ever Abrams does too. Lily is reckless and fearless. Ever is cautious and follows the rules. Lily wants to leave boring, rural Ryland and explore the world. Ever wants to stay in quiet, safe Ryland for the rest of her life. Lily was killed eighteen years ago while trying to solve her friend's murder. Ever is Lily reborn, and now she will have to break every rule and face every fear to find Lily's killer—before he kills her twice. From Clara Kensie, author of the RITA® award-winning Deception So series and the critically-acclaimed Aftermath, comes KILL ME ONCE, KILL ME TWICE: a dual-timeline, dual-romance, dual-mystery/thriller with a touch of magical realism for fans of The Walls Around Us and Vanishing Girls.

Find these books and more at

https://www.snowywingspublishing.com/books

www.ingramcontent.com/pod-product-compliance
Lightning Source LLC
Chambersburg PA
CBHW021326190726
48288CB00003B/983